Mills
Best Seller Romance

A chance to read and collect some of the best-loved novels
from Mills & Boon—the world's largest publisher of
romantic fiction.

Every month, six titles by favourite Mills & Boon authors
will be re-published in the *Best Seller Romance* series.

A list of other titles in the *Best Seller Romance* series
can be found at the end of this book.

Anne Mather

LOREN'S BABY

MILLS & BOON LIMITED
LONDON · TORONTO

First published 1978
Australian copyright 1978
Philippine copyright 1978
This edition 1983

© Anne Mather 1978

ISBN 0 263 74528 7

Set in Linotype Granjon 10 on 12 pt.
02–1283

Made and printed in Great Britain by
Richard Clay (The Chaucer Press) Ltd,
Bungay, Suffolk

CHAPTER ONE

The road widened at the top of the hill, as though inviting visitors to Port Edward to get out of their cars and take a look at the view before plunging down the narrow, precipitous lanes which eventually ran between the whitewashed cottages of the village. Telling herself it was because she wanted to see the village too, and not because it would provide a welcome delay to the culmination of her journey, Caryn thrust open the car door and climbed out.

Below, the sun-dappled roofs of Port Edward seemed too closely woven to allow for the passage of traffic, and beyond, the mud flats of the Levant estuary were exposed as the tide ebbed. An assortment of fishing vessels and pleasure craft were beached like so many gasping porpoises at their moorings, and children beach-combed in the shallow pools left stranded by the tide.

The road to the village said 'Port Edward only' and Caryn glanced about her thoughtfully. The address had said Port Edward too, but she remembered once Loren had told her that the house faced a creek where Tristan Ross kept his boat. If only she had paid more attention to those fleeting references to Druid's Fleet; but then she had never expected to have to come here. And didn't she also remember that there were trees? A house standing among trees . . .

The cliffs that overlooked the estuary were not thickly wooded, but further upstream Caryn could see forests of pine and spruce clinging staunchly to the hillside. Obviously she had come too far towards the village. She would have to turn the car and go back to where the road from Carmarthen had forked across the river.

It was easier said than done, but the road at this hour of
the evening was practically deserted, and she at last managed
to manoeuvre herself back the way she had come. She felt
tired, and half wished she had come by train, but it would
have been awkward asking a taxi driver to bring her to the
house and then expect him to wait while she saw Tristan
Ross. Particularly when there was always the chance that he
might not be at home. But Loren had said . . . Besides, if she
was truly honest with herself she would admit that her tired-
ness had more to do with her mental than her physical state,
and until she had this interview with Tristan Ross over, she
was not likely to feel much better.

She sighed. Was she making a mistake? she wondered for
the umpteenth time. Ought she to go through with this?
Could she go through with it? And then she remembered
Loren's face as she had last seen her, the cheekbones exposed
and skeletal in her thin face, her eyes hollow and haunted.
Her features had relaxed in death, but she would always
remember her pain and despair. *Always*.

She came to the fork that led across a narrow suspension
bridge shared by a disused railway line, and drove swiftly
across it, glancing at her wristwatch as she did so. It was
after six, but it had taken longer than she expected, and if
Tristan Ross was put out by her late arrival, there was
nothing she could do. Perhaps she should have driven into
the village after all and asked for directions. But she was
loath to draw attention to herself, particularly in the circumstances, and surely she was on the right track now.

The village was in sight again, but across the river now,
and Caryn drove more slowly, watching for any sign which
might indicate a dwelling of some kind. She saw a sign that
said 'Water's Reach' and pulled a wry face. Why couldn't

that have been Druid's Fleet? How much further did she
have to go?

After reaching a point which at a lower level precisely
matched the point she had reached on the opposite bank, she
stood on her brakes and chewed viciously at her lower lip.
She was getting nowhere, and not particularly fast. Where
the devil was the house? She couldn't have missed it. There
simply wasn't another house in sight.

Another three-point turn, and she was facing back the way
she had come once more. Below her, in the estuary, the tide
was beginning to turn, and ripples of water set the smaller
craft stirring on their ropes. The sun was sinking steadily
now, and a cool breeze drifted through the open window of
the car. It would be dark soon, she thought crossly, and she
was sitting here watching the tide come in as if she had all
the time in the world.

Putting the engine into gear again, she drove forward and
with a feeling of inevitability brought the car to a halt at the
stone posts supporting the sign 'Water's Reach'. There was
nothing else for it; she would have to ask directions. Surely
whoever owned Water's Reach would know where Druid's
Fleet could be found.

Beyond the gateposts, the drive sloped away quickly between pine trees, and with a shrug she locked the car and
with her handbag slung over one shoulder, descended the
steep gradient. She could see the roof of a house between the
branches of the trees, and as she got nearer she saw it was
a split-level ranch-style building whose stonework blended
smoothly into its backdrop of fir and silver spruce. A porch
provided shelter as she rang the bell, and she stood back
from the entrance as she waited, admiring the view away to
the right where the dipping rays of the sun turned the sails
of a yacht on the horizon to orange flames of colour. Only

the wind was a little chilly now, striking through the fine wool of her violet jersey suit.

The door had opened without her being aware of it; and she turned to face cold grey eyes set beneath darkly-arched brows. Expertly streaked blonde hair was drawn smoothly into a chignon on the nape of the woman's neck, while the elegant navy overall she wore bore witness to the fact that she had been interrupted while she was baking.

'Oh, I beg your pardon.' Caryn hid her nervousness in a smile. 'I wonder if you can help me.' The woman, Caryn guessed she must be about thirty, said nothing, just continued to stare inquiringly at her, and she hurried on: 'I'm looking for a house called—Druid's Fleet. Do you——'

'Who is it, Marcia?'

The impatient male voice from somewhere inside the house was vaguely familiar, and the woman turned automatically towards the sound. Caryn, half afraid she was about to close the door in her face, exclaimed: 'I'm so sorry if I've come at an inconvenient moment, but——'

She broke off abruptly as a man appeared behind the woman. For a moment she was too shocked to do anything but stare at him, but perhaps he was used to the effect his appearance had on girls. And why not? Those harshly etched sardonic features, vaguely haggard in appearance, were apparently capable of mesmerising his viewers, and Loren had told her he got more mail than any other interviewer in his field. For all that, he was taller than she had expected, and his lean body showed no signs as yet of the dissipations he indulged in, and considering she knew he was at least forty, his corn-fair hair showed little sign of grey. Of course, he was deeply tanned from his last assignment in East Africa, the one Loren had kept all those cuttings about, and his hair was no doubt bleached by the sun, thus disguising any unwelcome signs of encroaching age, but in his dark mohair business suit, he didn't look a day over thirty-five.

Recovering herself, Caryn realised both he and the woman were looking at her now, and colouring hotly, she said: 'Mr Ross?' annoyed to find her voice trembled a little as she spoke.

'Yes?' He sounded impatient now, and she felt resentful that he should. After all, she had not expected to find him *here*. Come to think of it, what was he doing here?

'I—I've been looking for your house, Mr Ross,' she said carefully, unwilling to say too much in front of the woman, and his expression suddenly changed.

'Hey!' he exclaimed, his impatience disappearing as swiftly as it had come. 'You're not from the agency, are you? My God! I never thought they'd send anyone so promptly.' He looked at his watch. 'Hell, I've got to be at the studios in half an hour. Can you wait till I get back?'

Caryn opened her mouth to protest that she was not from any agency, and then closed it again. Why not, if it served the purpose? She could easily explain her subterfuge when they spoke privately together.

'Druid's Fleet?' she ventured, avoiding a direct reply, and he shook his head.

'This is Druid's Fleet,' he explained apologetically. 'I guess you saw the old sign on the gatepost. I keep that there to discourage unwelcome sightseers. That's who we thought you were.'

'Oh.'

Caryn was taken aback, and the woman, Marcia, gave Ross a curious look. Then Tristan Ross was inviting her in, and feeling only slightly guilty, Caryn stepped inside.

She found herself in a large open hall, with stairs leading

both down and up. The floor was polished here, heavy wood blocks with a gleaming patina, that were an attractive foil for the skin rugs that enhanced its aura of age. There was an antique chest supporting a bowl of creamy yellow roses, and matching silk curtains billowed in the breeze beside the archway that led through to the dining room.

As Caryn followed Tristan Ross down the steps which led into the main body of the house, she was aware of Marcia coming behind her, and speculated on her relationship to the master of the house. His girl-friend, perhaps; or his mistress, she mused rather bitterly. He seemed to like to have a woman about the place. Loren had discovered that.

He led the way into a magnificent sitting room with long windows that looked out over the estuary. A padded window seat invited relaxation, or there were two squashy velvet couches, one either side of the stone fireplace, matching the heavy apricot velvet of the floor-length curtains. A coffee-coloured carpet fitted every corner, and the casual tables set around the room in no way encroached upon the feeling of space the room engendered.

Ross halted in the middle of the room and turned to face her. 'Have you eaten?'

Caryn shook her head, but hastened to add that she wasn't particularly hungry.

'Nonsense,' he exclaimed. 'Marcia will see you get something that appeals to you, and I'll be back in about two hours. I'm sorry about this, but I did warn the agency——'

'It's all right, really.' Caryn didn't want to get involved in discussions about the agency right now. 'I—I don't mind waiting.'

'Very well.' He raised his eyes to Marcia who was standing in the doorway. 'Can I leave it to you to see that

Miss—Miss——' He shook his head. 'I'm sorry, you didn't give me your name.'

Caryn thought quickly. 'Er—Mellor,' she got out jerkily. 'Susan Mellor.'

She thought his eyes narrowed for a moment, but then he was walking swiftly across the room again, past her to the door. 'Look after Miss Mellor, will you, Marcia?' she heard him say quietly, and then she heard him mount the steps again to the front door. It closed behind him a few moments later, and she was alone with her unwilling hostess.

The silence that followed his departure was broken only by Caryn smoothing moistened palms down her skirt. Then she faced Marcia with an apologetic smile.

'There's really no need to go to any trouble on my account. I—er—I honestly am not very hungry.'

Marcia considered her silently, and it was unnerving. What was wrong with the woman? Caryn thought impatiently. Why didn't she *say* anything?

'Have you lived here long?' she asked, and then realising how pointed that sounded, added: 'I mean—it's a very beautiful place to live, isn't it? I love Wales. I used to come here as a child. We used to camp on the Gower peninsula . . .'

Marcia inclined her head, as if in acknowledgement of Caryn's words, and then turned and walked away, across the lower hall and down two steps and through another door. Leading where? Caryn wondered. The kitchen, probably. What a taciturn creature she was! As if she couldn't have said something!

Left to herself, she relaxed somewhat. Well, she was here, and she was within reach of her goal. Or at least within sight of it. And she had been given two hours grace to augment her defences.

She walked across to the windows and admired the view. Then her eyes dropped to the terraced garden that fell away beneath her, and to the wooden flight of steps which led down to the boathouse. Loren had said there were thirty-seven steps, and she had had plenty of time to count them. Dangerous for a child perhaps, but that was not her problem.

Dropping her handbag on to the padded chocolate-brown cushions of the window seat, she half knelt beside it, feeling the familiar pang as she remembered what Loren had suffered. Why should he get away scot free?

She had been kneeling there for some time, hardly aware of the light fading until the switching on of a lamp brought her round with a start. Marcia had re-entered the room in that silent way of hers, and in her hands she carried a tray.

'Oh, you shouldn't have bothered!' Caryn exclaimed, sliding off the window seat, as Marcia set the tray down on one of the low tables nearby. But the smell of minestrone and fresh salmon was delectable, and she looked down on the meal the woman had prepared for her with undisguised gratitude.

Marcia spread her hands, and Caryn felt the guilt of false pretences colouring her cheeks once more. 'I say—won't you join me?'

Marcia shook her head. Her expression seldom altered, and Caryn was perplexed. Unless the woman *couldn't* speak, of course. But she must be able to hear. She had answered the doorbell, hadn't she? Yet how could she broach such a suggestion?

Marcia withdrew again, and with a shrug of defeat, Caryn seated herself on the couch beside the tray. She was hungry, she realised that now, and she remembered the old adage about fighting better on a full stomach.

But as she ate, she couldn't help wishing she had been able to ring Bob and Laura before coming here. It was going to be so late now before she got back to the hotel in Carmarthen, and she hoped they wouldn't worry. Still, he was in good hands, and that was the main thing.

Marcia reappeared with coffee as Caryn was finishing sampling the delights of a chocolate pudding. She had shed her overall to reveal a plain tailored grey dress, and looked more than ever like the lady of the house. Perhaps she was, thought Caryn doubtfully. Perhaps she should find out before Tristan Ross got back.

'That was absolutely delicious,' she said now, wiping her mouth on a napkin. 'Did you make the minestrone yourself? I've never tasted anything nicer.'

Marcia nodded, and retrieved the tray after setting down the coffee pot beside it. She was about to withdraw again, and on impulse Caryn got to her feet.

'Please,' she said. 'Don't rush away on my account.'

But Marcia's thin lips merely twitched slightly before she bowed her head and went away.

Caryn subsided on to the couch again. If Marcia wasn't dumb she was giving a damn good imitation of being so. She sighed, and reached for the coffee pot. Oh, well! If she didn't want to talk, she didn't want to talk. And maybe it was as well. She didn't want to get involved here—not more than necessary, anyway.

Her coffee finished, she looked about her restlessly. There was no television, which was unusual. She would have expected him to have one in every room. Was he on this evening? Was that why he had had to leave for the studios in Carmarthen? Or was it simply a pre-recording for something that was going out later?

Getting to her feet, she wandered round the large room. It

was a man's room, she thought reluctantly. There were no
ornaments to speak of, no china cabinet or collection of
porcelain in sealed cases. There were bookshelves, but she
couldn't believe anyone actually read such heavy, boring
tomes, and she longed for the sight of a paperback or a
magazine, anything to fill the time until Tristan Ross returned.

A silver trophy on the mantelshelf turned out to be an
award from the Television Academy of Arts and Sciences for
his contributions to the popular news programme *Action
World*, and beside it was a bronze shield denoting Tristan
Ross as Outstanding Television Correspondent for 1976.

Caryn pulled a face and put the awards down again,
wondering in passing whether a silver trophy would smash
if it fell into the stone hearth. It probably would, but she was
not brave enough to find out. She could imagine her stam-
mering apology: 'I—I'm s-sorry, Mr Ross. It—it just
s-slipped out of m-my f-fingers . . .'

Outside darkness had fallen, and she went to take another
look over the estuary. The lights of the village were comforting across the water, and here and there a mooring light
winked on the rising tide. A person could get delusions of
grandeur living here, she thought cynically. Remote from
the problems of the world outside.

The sound of a car's engine broke the stillness, and
although she hadn't heard him leave, Caryn guessed her host
had returned. She glanced at her watch. Eight-thirty. She
raised her dark eyebrows. He was prompt anyway; she
should be thankful for small mercies.

A door slammed, and then surprisingly, a female voice
called: 'Marcia! Marcia, I'm back! Whose car is that parked
at our gate? I almost ran into the wretched thing!'

Caryn stiffened. Another visitor? Someone well-used to

coming here anyway. Who else had a key to the door? Her lips tightened as she thought again of Loren's waxen features. Oh, Tristan Ross had such a rude awakening coming to him!

Light footsteps ran down the stairs, and a moment later a girl appeared in the open doorway—tall, slim, almost as tall as Caryn, in fact, who always considered her five feet eight inches to be less than an advantage, with straight fair hair and smooth pale skin. She was one of the most attractive young women Caryn had seen for some time, and her orange jump suit accentuated the slender grace of her figure while exposing more of the unblemished skin than was absolutely necessary.

She stopped short when she saw the other girl, and stared at her frowningly. Competition? wondered Caryn dryly, although she felt positively gipsy-dark beside such Scandinavian fairness. She tanned easily, and her skin was already brown, its texture caring nothing for the burning heat of the sun. She guessed this girl would have to be careful, or she would burn all too easily. And she probably was, Caryn conceded. She looked as if she spent some time caring for her appearance.

'Who are you?' she demanded now, and relieved to find someone who was not averse to speaking with her, Caryn answered:

'Susan—Mellor. I—I'm waiting to see Mr Ross.'

The girl frowned and came into the room. 'Why?'

It was a leading question, and Caryn hesitated. She had no qualms about evading an answer, but she was curious to know who the girl was, and antagonising her was not going to help. In consequence she gave the answer Ross himself had suggested:

'The—er—agency sent me.'

'The agency!'

The girl stared at her, and Caryn realised in dismay that if the next question was 'What agency?' she was stumped. What sort of agency might a man like Ross have contacted? Hysterical humour bubbled in her throat. She ought to be hoping it was as innocent as it sounded.

But the girl said: 'Do you mean the Llandath Agency?' and that was even worse.

Crossing her fingers behind her back, Caryn nodded. 'That's right,' she agreed manfully. 'The Llandath Agency.'

'You *liar!*'

It was worse than Caryn had imagined. The girl was staring at her unpleasantly, and what was worse, the woman Marcia had come to reinforce the opposition.

'Tris asked me to call at the agency,' the girl declared, glancing round at Marcia for her support. 'And I forgot! So what the hell do you think you're doing here? Are you a reporter or something? Or just one of those awful groupies?'

'I'm not a groupie!' exclaimed Caryn, fighting a ridiculous desire to laugh at the ludicrousness of the situation.

'What are you, then? Because I'm damn sure you're not a secretary!'

Caryn straightened her shoulders. 'As a matter of fact, you're wrong. I am a secretary,' she stated, more calmly than she felt. 'And—and Mr Ross—rang the agency.'

Half of it was true anyway, she consoled herself, but the girl wasn't finished yet. 'Tris wouldn't do that. Not when he'd asked me to call. Why should he? He knew I'd be in Carmarthen all afternoon.'

'Perhaps you'd better take that up with him,' remarked Caryn equably, and then started as a masculine voice said:

'Take what up with me? Angel, what's going on here? Why are you arguing with Miss Mellor?'

Tristan Ross came into the room. At some point on his journey home he had loosened his tie and unfastened the top button of his shirt, but he still managed to look calm and unruffled. Caryn noticed that contrary to tradition, the bottom button of his waistcoat was fastened, but his jacket was unfastened. Raking back the thick straight hair that was inclined to fall across his forehead, he regarded the two antagonists wryly, waiting for an explanation, and Caryn waited for 'Angel' to act entirely out of character.

'I didn't go to the agency, Tris!' she declared. 'I don't know what this woman's doing here, but she's not from Llandath.'

Caryn silently acknowledged the girl's attempt to classify her. Angel, if that really was her name, was younger than she was, but twenty-four didn't exactly put one in the middle-aged bracket.

Tristan Ross had listened expressionlessly to what Angel said, and now he turned to Caryn. 'Is that right? Are you not from the Llandath Agency?'

'I never said I was,' Caryn ventured slowly, and then when Angel began to protest, added: 'Not to you anyway. You—just—assumed that.'

His mouth turned down only slightly at the corners. 'All right, I'll assume some more. You chose not to enlighten me because you wanted to get in here, is that right?'

'Oh, I'd have got in here, Mr Ross,' declared Caryn levelly, 'whether you assumed I was from the agency or not.'

'Is that so?'

She barely acknowledged the edge of steel that deepened his voice now. 'Yes, that is so.'

'I see.' He glanced frowningly at the two other women. Then: 'You sound very sure of yourself, Miss—Mellor, is it? Or is that assumed, too?'

To her annoyance, Caryn coloured again. 'Yes, as a matter of fact it is. My name is Stevens, Caryn Stevens. Loren Stevens' sister.'

She watched him carefully as she said her sister's name, but it aroused no great reaction. A flicker of his eyes was all the notice he gave it, and then he shrugged and said:

'Forgive me, but I'm afraid I don't see the connection. Why should the sister of a girl who left my employ more than six months ago want to see me? Or are you looking to take over your sister's position?'

Caryn gasped. 'How dare you!'

At last she aroused some reaction, and the thin lips tightened ominously. 'How dare I?' he demanded harshly. 'Come, Miss Stevens. I think this has gone far enough. Either tell me what in damnation you want or get out of here!'

Caryn gazed at the two women watching them so intently. 'I would rather say what I have to say in private,' she declared unevenly.

'Would you?' He made no attempt to dismiss their audience. 'Well, I wouldn't. Whatever it is, spit it out. Here! Where I have some witnesses.'

Caryn licked her lips. This was not what she had intended. She shrank from exposing her sister before two strangers. It was bad enough having to tell him. She could not bring herself to speak the words in front of anyone else.

'I—I can't,' she said at last. 'I—I won't.'

Tristan Ross's teeth ground together. 'Miss—Miss Stevens: I don't know why you've come here, but I should tell you that I have no secrets from either my daughter or my housekeeper.'

'Your—your daughter!' Caryn swallowed convulsively.

'Angel—Angela. Angela Ross. Didn't your sister tell you about her?'

'No.'

'Or about Marcia?'

'No.'

'You don't have to worry about her carrying tales, or isn't that what's troubling you?'

So the woman couldn't speak! Caryn felt a rush of sympathy, but then she gathered her small store of confidence about her. She straightened her spine, but even in her wedged heels he topped her by several inches, which was a disadvantage, she found. However, she had to go on:

'Mr Ross,' she said slowly, 'what I have to say concerns my sister, not me. Please——' She hated having to beg. 'Give me a few minutes of your time.'

Impatience hardened his lean features. 'Miss Stevens, I've just spent an uncomfortable half hour interviewing a man who refuses to admit that he's a bloody Communist, and I'm tired! I'm not in the mood for play-acting or over-dramatisation, and if this has something to do with Loren then I guess it's both——'

Caryn's hand jerked automatically towards his cheek, and he made no attempt to stop her. The sound of her palm rang in the still room, and only his daughter's protest was audible.

Tristan Ross just hooked his thumbs into the back waistband of his trousers under his jacket and heaved a heavy sigh. 'Is that all?' he enquired flatly, but Angela burst out:

'Are you going to let her get away with that?' in shocked tones.

In truth, Caryn was as confused as the other girl. The blow administered, she was disarmed, and they all knew it.

With a sense of futility, she would have brushed past him

and made for the door, but his hand closed round her arm, preventing her from leaving.

'Not so fast,' he said, and she noticed inconsequently how the red weals her fingers had left in no way detracted from the disturbing attraction of his dark features. Such unusually dark features with that light hair. The hair he had obviously bestowed on his daughter. *His daughter!* For heaven's sake, why hadn't Loren mentioned that he had a grown-up daughter? Did he have a wife, too? Was that why . . .

'Where do you think you're going?' he demanded, and she held up her head.

'I—I'll write to you,' she said, saying the first thing that came into her head, and he stared at her frustratedly.

'Why? What have we to say to one another? If Loren has something to say why the hell didn't she come and say it herself?'

Caryn's jaw quivered. 'Loren is dead, Mr Ross. Didn't you know?'

At last she had succeeded in pricking his self-confidence. His hand fell from her arm as if it burned him, and feeling the blood beginning to circulate through that numbed muscle once more, Caryn felt a trembling sense of awareness. She was too close to him, she thought faintly. She could almost share his shock of cold disbelief, feel the wave of revulsion that swept over him.

'*Dead!*' he said incredulously. 'Loren—dead? My God, I'm sorry. I had no idea.'

'Why be sorry?' Angela spoke again. 'She was nothing but a nuisance all the time she was here——'

'*Angel!*'

His harsh interjection was ignored as Caryn added bitterly: 'Why pretend to be sorry, Mr Ross? You never answered any of her letters.'

'Her letters?' He shook his head. 'All right, Miss Stevens, you've won. We'll go into my study. We can talk privately there——'

'You're not going to talk to her, are you?' Angela's dismayed protest rang in their ears, but Tristan Ross just looked at his daughter before walking past her out of the room.

Caryn hesitated only a moment before following him. This was what she wanted, wasn't it? Why then did she feel so little enthusiasm for the task?

They went across the hall and down a passage that descended by means of single steps at intervals to an even lower level, and he thrust open a leather-studded door and stood back to allow her to precede him inside.

The room was only slightly smaller than the living room, with all the books Caryn could have wished for lining the walls. Paperbacks there were in plenty, as well as every issue of the *Geographical Magazine* for years past. A honey-brown carpet supported a leather-topped desk, a pair of revolving leather chairs, and several armchairs. A smaller desk in one corner held a typewriter and a pair of wire trays, with metal filing cabinets completing the furnishings. Here again, the windows overlooked the estuary, but it was dark and Ross drew the venetian blinds.

'Won't you sit down?' he suggested, indicating one of the armchairs, but Caryn preferred to stand. 'As you wish.' He took off his jacket and draped it over the back of one of the leather chairs. 'But if you'll excuse me . . .'

'Of course.'

He lounged into one of the revolving chairs, behind the desk, and in spite of his informal attire he was still the Tristan Ross she knew from so many current affairs programmes. Calm, polite, faintly sardonic; using his grammar school education to its fullest potential while still maintaining the common touch that encouraged the most unlikely people to confide in him.

'Right,' he said, and she thought rather hysterically that all that was missing were the television cameras. 'Suppose you tell me why you wanted to see me.'

Taking a deep breath, she decided to come straight to the point. 'You—knew about Loren, didn't you?'

'What did I know?'

He was annoyingly oblique, and she clenched her fists. 'She wrote and told you about—about the baby——'

'The baby!' His indolence disappeared. 'What baby?'

Caryn suddenly found she had to sit down after all, and backed until her knees came up against the soft velvety cushioning of an armchair. She sat down rather weakly on the edge of the seat.

'I said—*what* baby?' he repeated, getting to his feet to rest the palms of his hands on the desk in front of him, leaning slightly towards her. 'I warn you—if this is another of Loren's tricks——'

'I told you. Loren's dead!' she reminded him tersely, and his jaw clenched.

'So you did.'

'Why didn't you answer any of her letters?'

'For God's sake! I don't remember seeing any letters from her. And even if I had——'

He broke off abruptly and Caryn guessed what he had been going to say. 'You wouldn't have answered them?'

'Look,' he sighed, 'Mrs Forrest—that's the name of the woman I employed on a temporary basis to take over after—after Loren left—she had orders to deal with—well, that sort of thing.'

'Fan mail?' demanded Caryn bitterly, and his eyes held hers coldly.

'Why not?' he challenged, and she wondered how she could have thought his eyes were dark. They were light, amber-coloured, the alert eyes of a prey-hunting animal at bay.

'She told you she was expecting *your* child and you ignor——'

'*She did what?*' He came round the desk towards her so violently that for a moment she thought he intended to strike her. But he halted just in time, staring down at her, the muscles of his face working tensely. 'Say that again!'

Caryn licked her dry lips. 'She—she was expecting your——'

'The bitch!'

Caryn came abruptly to her feet. 'Don't you dare to speak of my sister like that!'

'I'll speak of her how the hell I like!' he retorted savagely. 'God Almighty, what a bloody cock-and-bull story that is! And you came here to tell me that——'

'Not just for that,' she got out jerkily. 'Not just for that.'

He made an effort to calm himself, but he began to pace about the room and she was reminded of a predator once more. He moved so lithely, so naturally; with all the grace and none of the nobility of the beast, she thought fiercely.

'Of course,' he said coldly. 'You came to tell me she was dead. Well, perhaps it's just as well.' He stopped to stare into her working features. 'Perhaps it's just as well. I think if she'd still been alive, I'd have killed her!'

Caryn backed off again. 'And—and what about your son?' she got out chokingly. 'What about him? Do you want to kill him, too?'

CHAPTER TWO

She saw the colour leave his face as he looked at her. Even his tan took on a jaundiced appearance, and she realised what a tremendous shock this must have been for him.

'My—son?' he echoed faintly. 'You mean—there's a child?'

'Y—yes. A boy. He's—three months old.'

'Three months!'

Close to her like this, his eyes had a curious magnetic quality, the pupils dilated so that the tawny irises were almost extinguished. His lashes were thick and straight, gold-tipped she saw, like the sun-bleached texture of his hair. Impatience and confusion twisted the firm contours of his mouth, depriving it of its normally sensual curve. She wondered fleetingly if the child would be like him, and then squashed the thought as being unworthy of speculation.

The silence between them was beginning to get to her, and she shifted uncomfortably under his gaze, suddenly aware of the pulse jerking at his jawline, the strong column of his throat rising above the opened neck of his shirt. In the warm room, redolent with the salty tang of the estuary, a hangover from opened windows on the sun-filled afternoon, she could still smell the faint heat of his body mingling with less personal scents of soap and after-shave. It made her aware of her own vulnerability, and she realised what a temptation he must have been to an impressionable girl like Loren.

'Three months,' he said again at last. Sarcasm curled his lips. 'Why wait so long?'

'Before coming here, you mean?' she asked jerkily.

'That's exactly what I do mean.' His fingers inserted themselves into the minute pockets of his waistcoat. 'Or was I last on the list?'

'You——'

Her instinctive response was to hit him once more, but he backed off mockingly, raising one hand to defend himself. 'Oh, no,' he said, shaking his head. 'Not again. We played that little scene ten minutes ago. Melodrama was never my strong point.'

'What is your strong point, Mr Ross?' she demanded hotly. 'Seducing teenagers?'

The bones of his cheeks were clearly visible as his breath was sucked in. Then, in cold denigrating tones, he said: 'Are you aware of the laws governing slander? If you would care to repeat those words in the presence of the other members of this household, I think I can promise you you'll find out.'

Caryn's lips trembled, but she had to go on. 'Do you deny seducing my sister, Mr Ross?'

He heaved a sigh. 'Would you believe me if I did?'

'No.'

'Then that's rather a pointless question, don't you think?'

Caryn sniffed. 'I might have known what kind of man you'd turn out to be.'

'So why did you come here?'

'Because that child is yours, and he's your responsibility!'

'Ah, I see.' He gave a harsh laugh. 'It's money you want.'

'*No!*' Caryn was horrified. 'You—you don't think I've come here to—to blackmail you, do you?'

'You used that word, not me.'

'But you—implied it.' She made a grimace of distaste. 'Oh, you're twisting all my words. You're making it so—so sordid!'

'And isn't it?' he snapped. 'Coming here, telling me some crazy story about your sister dying and insinuating that it was my fault——'

'It was!'

'Oh, no.' He shook his head. 'If your sister's dead, it has nothing to do with me.'

Caryn forced herself to meet his eyes. 'How can you say that? You must have known there was a risk——'

'What risk?' he grated. 'For God's sake, I didn't know she was pregnant!'

Caryn tried to be calm. 'You must have known she might be,' she insisted. 'You left her to tell her family——'

'Her family!' He raised his eyes heavenward for a moment as if seeking patience. 'I didn't even know she had a family, until you came here purporting to be her sister.'

'I am her sister.'

'Very well. And I was her employer. Her *employer*! Do you understand? I seldom discuss personal matters with employees unless they impinge in some way upon the working capacity of the employee concerned. Is that clear enough for you?'

Caryn tried again: 'But your relationship with Loren was more than that of employer-employee.'

'Was it?'

'Well, wasn't it?'

'Did she tell you that it was?'

'I didn't need to be told,' Caryn declared tremulously. 'She was mad about you.'

'Really?' He was unmoved. 'And I was mad about her, too, I suppose.'

'For a while . . .'

'For a while!' He brought his balled fist hard into the

palm of his hand. 'My God, I can't believe anyone could be that—that——'

'Gullible?' she supplied coldly, but he snapped: 'No! *Stupid!*'

'Loren was not stupid,' she protested, and his lips sneered:

'Did I say Loren?' he taunted, and her fists clenched.

'You think you're so clever, don't you, Mr Ross?'

'No.' He shook his head irritably. 'Not clever at all. I was stupid. I knew what she was the minute I saw her. I should never have taken her on.'

Caryn couldn't permit this. 'Loren was a good secretary——'

'There are thousands of good secretaries.'

'She was loyal. She worked hard.'

'She made life impossible!' he muttered.

'You admit then that your relationship with her wasn't as platonic as you would have me think——'

'I admit nothing,' he declared, turning his back on her and walking back to his desk. 'Nothing!'

Caryn drew in a long breath and expelled it unsteadily. 'So you deny that the child is yours?'

There was silence for a moment and then he turned and rested back against the side of his desk, one hand on either side of him supporting his body. 'Tell me about the child,' he said. 'Tell me how she died.'

Caryn sought for words. 'I—she—when you fired her——' She waited for him to deny this, but when he didn't, she went on: 'When you fired her, she came back to London. To—the flat.'

'Your parents' flat?' he inquired.

'No. Mine.' Caryn hesitated, then she went on: 'Our parents are dead. We were brought up in Maidstone by an elderly aunt, but when I was old enough, I left there to take a commercial course in London. Then when Loren was older, she did the same.'

'And you shared the flat?'

'Well, it was my flat really. Loren wasn't there all the time. She had . . . friends . . .'

'Friends?'

'Yes, friends.' Caryn saw no point in revealing that Loren had always preferred the company of men to women. 'Anyway, later on she got this job, down here—living in. I—I advised her not to take it.'

'Why not?' He was curious.

'Because of you. Because of your reputation,' declared Caryn firmly.

'What reputation?' he pursued tautly.

Caryn was discomfited. 'Does it matter?'

'Yes, I think it does.'

She sighed. 'You know what I mean as well as I do.'

'You shouldn't believe all you read in the papers, Miss Stevens,' he retorted.

'Obviously not,' she flared. 'They omitted to mention that you were married.'

'My wife died when Angela was three. Does that absolve me from that particular crime?'

Caryn flushed. 'It's nothing to do with me.'

'Is any of this?'

'Yes. I—I was with Loren when she died.'

He hunched his shoulders. 'Go on. When did she tell you she was pregnant?'

Caryn hesitated. 'Not for some time. She—she was so thin, you see. It—hardly showed.'

He frowned. 'Did she get another job?'

'No.' Caryn was reluctant to tell everything that happened

those last few months, but perhaps she owed him that, at least. 'She—as you know, there are not that many jobs around. And—and she was—listless, without enthusiasm. She said she had written to you and asked you to take her back again.'

'She knew I was going to East Africa.'

'Yes. She collected all the cuttings.'

'My God!' He sounded disgusted.

'But she wrote to you after you got back. As I said before, you never replied.'

'I told Mrs Forrest to ignore those letters. I knew what Loren was like. I knew she wouldn't give up that easily.'

'She depended on you . . .'

'She was a leech!'

'She was so happy here to begin with. She used to write such excited letters, telling me how you used to take her with you on certain assignments——'

'I took her once,' he declared heavily.

'Nevertheless, you took advantage of her.'

'I did what?'

'She told me how—how you used to—to pester her——'

'What?' He stared at her incredulously.

'—coming home drunk after parties. Forcing your attentions upon her——'

'Is that what she told you?'

'Of course.'

'And you believed it?'

'Why not? Loren didn't lie about things like that.'

'Didn't she?'

'I suppose you used to get her drunk, too,' Caryn accused him. 'Was that how you got into her bed?'

'Oh, my God!' His face twisted. 'Do you think I'd have to do that to sleep with her?' He shook his head.

'I don't believe you.'

He shrugged. 'Unlike your sister, I cannot arouse your sympathy or your trust.' He gave a bitter smile. 'But we're straying from the point, aren't we? You still haven't told me why you're here.'

'I should have thought that was obvious.'

'Well, I'm sorry. It's not.'

'I've told you. The child is your responsibility now.'

'In what way?'

'You're his father. You should support his upbringing.'

'Financially? Or physically?'

'What do you mean?'

'Are you asking for money or aren't you, Miss Stevens?'

Caryn paused. 'Loren—Loren told me to come to you. To bring the child to you. She said—she said you would know what to do.'

He stared at her disbelievingly. 'And you accepted that?'

'Why shouldn't I?'

'After what she had told you about me?'

Caryn shook her head. 'That has nothing to do with it.'

'I disagree. It has everything to do with it. What does a man like me want with an innocent child? A man who goes around seducing teenagers? A man, moreover, who you have just accused of introducing your sister to drink!'

'He's your son,' insisted Caryn doggedly, refusing to be alarmed.

'And your nephew. Or had you overlooked that?'

'It's nothing to do with me,' Caryn exclaimed restlessly. 'It's not my child.'

His amber eyes narrowed. 'You sound very vehement about it. Don't you like children?'

'It killed my sister, Mr Ross. Do you think I can forget that?'

'Ah, I see.' He sounded sardonic. 'How convenient! Shift the blame—and the responsibility.'

'I have to work for my living, Mr Ross. I don't have time to take care of a baby.'

'It may have slipped your notice, Miss Stevens, but I work for my living, too.'

'That's different.'

'How different?'

'You—you have money . . .'

'I see. So it is money you want,' he mocked coldly.

'*No!*'

'Why should I believe you? How do I know you're not making the whole thing up? You're Loren's sister! Maybe you're in this together!'

Her white face seemed to sober him, and he muttered a rough apology: 'Okay, I'm sorry. I didn't mean that. You're nothing like her, thank God!'

Caryn's throat felt tight. 'Loren is dead.'

'Yes, yes, so you keep telling me.'

'It's true!'

'I believe it.' He expelled his breath on a long sigh. 'So: where is the kid?'

'In London. Spending the day with some friends who live in the adjoining flat to mine. Laura—that's the girl's name—she's expecting a baby herself in three months.'

'Really.' He sounded uninterested, and she wished she hadn't volunteered the information. She had only wanted to assure him that the child was in good hands. 'How soon can I see him?'

'You mean—you mean you'll have him?' Suddenly it all seemed totally unreal.

'You're prepared to give him away, aren't you? To a complete stranger?'

'You're his father,' she protested, but he shook his head.

'You can't prove that.'

'You can't prove you're not.'

'I wouldn't be too sure of that, if I were you.'

'Oh, please!' Caryn's cry was ragged. 'Will you or won't you take him?'

'Let's say I want to examine the goods first, hmm?' He paused. 'Does he have a name?'

'Yes.' Caryn was reluctant to admit it. 'Loren called him Tristan, but I—I——'

'You couldn't bring yourself to use it, is that it?' he questioned dryly.

'Maybe.'

He began to pace again, measuring the room with his lean, pantherlike strides. 'So—where do you live?'

'I can drive back and fetch him——'

'No.' He halted once more. 'No, don't do that. I'll come to London. You'd better give me your address.'

Caryn was loath to do so. 'I can easily bring him here.'

'I'm sure you can,' he agreed, 'but I prefer to do it my way.'

'You can't pay me off!' she burst out uncontrollably, and his lips curled.

'I don't intend to.'

A knock at the study door curtailed any response she might have made, and without waiting for his summons, Angela Ross appeared in the doorway. Her eyes flickered over Caryn without liking, and then she looked at her father.

'Tris, how much longer are you going to be? Marcia's made a pizza for your supper, and it's going to be ruined if you don't eat it soon.'

His features changed as he looked at his daughter. Watching him, Caryn felt a curious pang at the gentleness of his expression. Why couldn't he have looked at Loren like that? she thought resentfully. Why should this girl feel herself so secure when he owed just as much allegiance to the woman who had borne his child, and to his son . . .

'We're almost through,' he told Angela now. 'Miss—er—Stevens is leaving.'

Caryn squared her shoulders. 'If you'll give me a sheet of paper, I'll give you my address.'

She was aware of his daughter's raised eyebrows, but she didn't care. Angela would have to know sooner or later, and why should she protect her? It was up to her father to explain, if he could.

Angela hung around as Caryn wrote her address on the pad he handed to her, adding her telephone number in case it was needed. Tristan barely glanced at it as he tossed it on to his desk, and she was aware that he was waiting for her to go.

'I'll be in touch,' he assured her politely, his eyes glinting with suppressed anger. She guessed he had not cared for her referring to some future association in front of his daughter, but that was just too bad, she thought half defensively.

Outside, the air had never smelt so sweet, and she walked up to where she had left the car on legs that threatened to give out on her. Well, she had done it, she thought defiantly, and wondered why she was suddenly so doubtful . . .

Caryn spent the night at the hotel in Carmarthen and travelled back to London the next morning. The journey seemed so much shorter going back, but perhaps that was because she had more enthusiasm towards her destination.

Her flat was on the second floor of a house in Bloomsbury. It was not the most fashionable area of London, but it was civilised, and the tall Victorian houses had an atmosphere that was missing from the stark concrete and glass sky-scrapers that had sprung up all around them. Mrs Theobald, who lived on the ground floor, had window boxes, and at this time of the year they were bright with geraniums, and gave a distinct individuality to Number 11 Faulkner Terrace. Caryn had rung her friends from the hotel that morning, and when she reached the second floor the door of the Westons' flat opened and Laura appeared with the baby in her arms.

'Hi,' she said, smiling, her freckled face showing sympathy for Caryn's aching legs. 'Come in and have a cuppa. Bob's already gone to the studio.'

Bob Weston was a commercial photographer, working for a small agency in Notting Hill. He photographed weddings and christenings, and occasionally did spreads for small magazines, but his ambition was to move into the more lucrative world of television.

'Thanks.' Caryn barely glanced at her nephew as she followed Laura into the flat, a facsimile of her own except that it was much tidier. She tried never to let herself feel any attachment for the child, knowing as she did that the authorities would not let her keep him much longer.

'He's been so good,' Laura exclaimed, closing the door before walking to a folding pram standing in the corner. 'He didn't even wake during the night.'

'No. He's very good.' Caryn sounded weary and indifferent, and Laura looked at her anxiously.

'Well?' she ventured. 'What happened? You were very vague on the phone this morning.'

Caryn flung herself into an armchair. 'I told you I saw—him.'

'Yes.' Laura padded through to the tiny kitchen to put on the kettle. 'But you didn't say what was going to happen.'

'He wants to see him.'

'Who?' Laura came to the door of the kitchen. 'Tristan Ross wants to see the baby?'

'Yes.'

Laura grimaced. 'So when are you taking him?'

'I'm not. He wants to come here.'

Laura ran a hand over the swelling mound of her stomach and subsided into a chair with evident relief. 'Heavens!'

Caryn forced à rueful smile. 'Yes. I'd better see about tidying my place up.'

'I didn't mean that. And besides, it isn't so bad.'

Caryn sighed. 'It isn't so good. But since Loren died . . . and having him . . .' She tipped her head towards the pram from which direction a low gurgling sound could be heard.

Laura shook her head uncomprehendingly. 'I don't know how you can consider giving him away,' she burst out unwillingly. 'He's adorable. And so sweet . . .'

'Oh, Laura!' Caryn shifted restlessly. 'How can I keep him? I don't earn enough to support him, for one thing. And who would look after him while I was at work? You can't much longer, and then . . .'

'But don't you love him?'

'There's not much point, is there?' murmured Caryn bitterly, getting up and walking across the room, coming to a halt reluctantly beside the folding pram. Of course he was sweet, she thought impatiently, as she saw the quiff of feathery fair hair, the plump little hands curling and uncurling, the softly pursed lips oozing dribbles down his chin. Laura was right—he was a good baby. But she had no time for babies.

The kettle whistled and Laura got up to make the tea, and returning to her seat Caryn reflected what good friends the Westons had been to her. Without their assistance, she could never have kept the baby this long, but she had been determined not to let the social services people take him. Not after what Loren had begged her to do.

And yet it hadn't been easy, making up her mind to go and see Tristan Ross. For one thing, she had had to find out where he lived and whether he was there at the moment. He spent quite a lot of his time travelling, but fortunately Bob had had connections in the television industry, and he had supplied the information that when Ross returned from his present trip to Canada he was scheduled to do a series of programmes for a London television company.

Laura carried the tray of tea into the living room and set it down on a table near at hand. Caryn came to join her, and they each enjoyed the reviving flavour of the beverage.

Munching a biscuit, which she confessed she should not be eating, Laura asked when Tristan Ross intended to come to the flat.

'I don't know,' Caryn admitted with a sigh. 'But I gave him the phone number. I guess he'll ring first and make an appointment. He's used to doing that sort of thing.'

'What was he like?'

Laura was intrigued, but Caryn just poured herself more tea and gave an offhand shrug of her shoulders. 'You know what he's like,' she said. 'You've seen him on television plenty of times.'

'I know.' Laura gave an embarrassed laugh. 'But it's different meeting someone, isn't it?'

'I'm not a fan,' declared Caryn flatly, and her friend's freckled face coloured unbecomingly.

'I know that,' she murmured uncomfortably. 'I didn't mean to suggest you were.'

'Oh, I'm sorry, Laura.' Caryn felt contrite. 'Take no notice of me. I'm an ungrateful creature. And after all you've done for me . . .' She made an effort to be objective. 'He—well, he's taller than you might imagine, and he's certainly—well, sexy, I suppose.'

'You could understand why Loren was so infatuated with him, then?' asked Laura quietly.

'Oh, yes.' Caryn had to be honest, although it went against the grain to find excuses for him. 'I should think she found him fascinating. Any—any impressionable woman would.'

'But not you?' suggested Laura dryly.

'*Me!*' Caryn looked affronted. 'You must be joking!'

'Why? That's quite a solution to your problems, have you thought of that?'

'What do you mean?'

Laura looked uncomfortable now. 'Well, I—I just meant—him being the baby's father, and you its aunt—perhaps you might——'

'Get together, you mean?' Caryn was horrified.

Laura's colour came and went, but she stuck to her guns. 'Well, why not? I mean, we all know—that is, you know Loren was prone to—exaggeration——'

'Laura, what are you saying?' Caryn stared at her. 'Don't you believe Tristan Ross is *his*——' she indicated the pram, '—his father?'

'Oh, yes.' Laura was quick to protest. 'I do, I do. Only—well, maybe it wasn't as—maybe she—wanted it, too.'

Caryn heaved a heavy sigh. 'I see.' She moved her shoulders wearily. 'Okay, I'll accept that perhaps Loren did—encourage him.' She lifted her head. 'What girl wouldn't, for heaven's sake?'

'You said you wouldn't,' Laura reminded her, and Caryn looked down into her teacup.

'I know I did. And I meant it. But anyway, that still doesn't change things. I think he sacked her when he suspected she was pregnant. Nothing can alter that. And when she wrote and told him, he ignored her letters.'

Laura nodded slowly. 'I suppose you're right.' Then she looked at her friend. 'I just can't help thinking that you're going to regret this.'

'What?'

'Giving—him away. Caryn, he is your nephew!'

'He's Tristan Ross's son. He can do a lot more for him than I can.'

'I can't argue with that.' Laura straightened her spine, wincing at her aching back. 'I just wish that was our baby lying in the pram there. Without all the effort of having him.'

Caryn grinned, relaxing a little. 'You don't mean that. You're loving every minute of it. I've never seen Bob so attentive.'

Laura smiled too. 'No,' she agreed happily. 'He has been marvellous, hasn't he? Do you know he went out the other night at half past eleven to get me some fish and chips?'

'Fish and chips! At half past eleven!' Caryn grimaced. 'Oh, Laura, how could you?'

Laura giggled. 'I don't know. I was ravenous, that's all. I had to eat fruit and crackers all the following day before I dared go to the clinic. I have to watch my blood pressure, you see.'

'And having junior over there isn't helping things, is it?' remarked Caryn dryly. 'Let's hope his—*daddy* comes for him soon.'

Laura looked at her anxiously. 'Let's hope so,' she sighed, but she didn't sound convincing.

CHAPTER THREE

Caryn worked in Cricklewood, and every morning she delivered her nephew into Laura's capable hands, collecting him again when she came home at five o'clock. It was an arrangement that had worked very well, except that Caryn felt guilty about taking advantage of Laura's good nature. Still, she did pay for the service, and Laura insisted they could do with the extra money with the baby on the way.

However, the arrangement did not do a lot for Caryn's social life. She worked as secretary to the Dean of Lansworth College, and during the course of her duties she was brought into contact with a lot of young men. But perhaps fortunately none of them had appealed to her seriously, and her most lasting admirer was the Dean himself.

Laurence Mellor was a man in his early fifties, still virile and attractive, with a broad muscular frame and iron grey hair. His wife had run off with a fellow colleague in his first years as assistant at Lansworth, but he had weathered the storm of gossip which had followed and had eventually been made head of the art college. His intense interest in his work had probably been responsible for the break-up of his marriage, Caryn had surmised, but since he had become Dean the pressure was off, and he had more time to think about his personal life.

Caryn had been his secretary for four years. She had come to Lansworth from a position in a typing pool with a firm of solicitors, but like Mellor himself, she had been ambitious, and he had recognised her determination as soon as he saw her. They got along well together, and on those occasions when he needed a hostess he always called on Caryn.

He knew of the affair with Loren, of course, although not all the personal details. He knew she had been Tristan Ross's secretary for a while, but he had not connected that with her subsequent pregnancy. When she died, he was sympathetic, and he always prided himself on being open-minded about things like that. Consequently he had not connected her sister with Caryn's request for two days' leave of absence to visit a sick relative in South Wales.

Caryn returned to the college on Thursday, and to her relief Laurence was out of the office all morning attending a governors' meeting. By the time he returned she was immersed in her duties and able to answer his enquiries without obvious embarrassment. Even so, she was taken aback when he came to perch his ample frame on the corner of her desk and said without warning:

'Have you decided yet what you're going to do about Loren's baby? I don't think I approve of you working all day and all night as well.'

Caryn finished fitting the wedge of typing paper into the machine to give herself time to recover, and then said casually: 'I don't work all night, Laurence.'

'No.' He fingered his tie thoughtfully. 'But you do look after him in the evenings, don't you? And there must be—nappies to wash. That sort of thing.'

He sounded as though such an occupation offended the fastidiousness of his nature, and she had to smile. 'There are nappies,' she agreed, 'but only wet ones. There are disposable pads on the market now, you know.'

'Nevertheless, you have very little free time these days,' he insisted. 'You can't go on like this, Caryn. It's not right. It's not as if the baby were yours.'

Caryn looked up into his broad expressive face. He was obviously concerned for her, but she couldn't help wonder-

ing if he had some occasion coming up when he would need
her assistance, and was sounding her out about babysitters.

'As a matter of fact, I don't plan to keep him much
longer,' she admitted slowly, and his face brightened con-
siderably.

'No?'

'No.' She hesitated. 'There's someone—someone I know,
who might—give him a home.'

'A relative?'

'Sort of.'

'I see.' Laurence looked much relieved. 'Well, I can't say
I'm not delighted, because I am.' He slid off the desk to
stand before her, taking his watch out of his fob pocket and
examining it absently. 'As a matter of fact, something's come
up, something I wanted to discuss with you. I was hoping
you might be able to have dinner with me.'

Caryn hid the wry acknowledgement of her suspicions, and
frowned consideringly. 'I don't think I could make it tonight, Laurence,' she said apologetically. 'I've been away a
couple of days, as you know, and I don't think I ought to ask
Laura to babysit again tonight. Maybe tomorrow . . .'

'It can wait another day,' Laurence agreed at once. 'Tomorrow evening it shall be. Where shall we eat? In town—
or out?'

'Wherever you like,' Caryn replied, quite looking forward
to the break from routine, and Laurence went away saying
he would think about it.

In fact they ate in town, at Beluccis in Soho, where
Laurence was a valued customer. The restaurant was small,
but not inexpensive, and a corner table was always found for
him. The lighting was subdued and intimate, and Caryn had
accompanied him there twice before.

He ordered Martinis, and then got straight to the point.

'I've been invited to the United States during the summer vacation,' he explained, and Caryn felt a twinge of interest. 'It's a tour of several university campuses, some lecturing, some studying. A kind of sabbatical, I suppose.' He paused as the waiter brought their drinks. 'But I don't want to go alone,' he went on, when they were alone again. 'I want you to come with me.'

'To the United States!' Caryn gasped. 'Laurence!'

'Well, why not? You're my secretary, aren't you?'

'Yes, but——'

'Ah, I see. You're worried about what people will say. I don't blame you. Colleges are notorious places for gossip.'

'It's not just that, Laurence. I mean—the expense . . .'

He put his drink aside and reached across the table to take one of her hands in his. This was something he had done before, too. When he wanted something, he could be as persuasive as the next man. But this time Caryn was disturbed by the light in his eyes.

'Caryn,' he said softly, 'have you ever thought of getting married?'

'Married?' She shook her head. 'Not seriously, no.'

'Never?'

'No.' She tried to make a joke of it, not liking the serious turn the conversation had taken. 'No one's asked me.'

'I can't believe that.'

'Well, no one I would want to marry,' she conceded lightly.

'Marry me, Caryn. Marry me!'

She withdrew her hand at once, pressing it close into the other in her lap. 'Laurence!' she exclaimed, realising she had been afraid of this happening. 'You're not serious.'

'I am. I am.' He sighed. 'Is it my age? Is that the barrier?'

'I don't love you, Laurence . . .'

'Love!' He scoffed at the word. 'What is love? I loved Cecily and look where it got me!' He shook his head. 'You think I'm too old, don't you?'

'Laurence, if I loved someone, I wouldn't care how old they were. Honestly.'

He refused to give up. 'You could learn to love me. I would teach you.'

'Why?' Caryn's brows ascended. 'Do you love me?'

He shifted restively. 'I've told you, I don't believe in that sort of emotional foolishness.' He pressed on: 'Caryn, we have so much in common. Our work, our liking for books and music . . .'

'It wouldn't work, Laurence. They're not good enough reasons for getting married!'

The waiter was hovering, waiting for their order, and somewhat impatiently Laurence suggested they chose what they planned to eat. But Caryn's appetite had been drastically reduced, and she insisted that an omelette with salad was all she wanted.

The waiter departed and Laurence returned to the attack. 'Very well,' he said levelly, 'if you won't marry me, at least come with me. I need you.'

'You need *someone*,' she corrected him quietly. 'And that's why I won't marry you, Laurence. Because I'm not just someone, I'm me! I don't want to spend my life as a cipher!'

He looked hurt. 'I think you're being unnecessarily harsh. If I've ever treated you that way, I'm sorry——'

'I'm not saying you have—yet. But if we were married . . . Oh, it's no use, Laurence. Let's forget it, shall we?'

'And the tour?'

'I don't know. I just don't know.'

He chewed at his lower lip. 'We could pretend to be

engaged. For the duration of the trip, I mean.'

Caryn laughed. 'You make it sound like the plot for a romantic novel! Honestly, I never believed people actually went in for that sort of thing.'

'What sort of thing?' he asked shortly.

'Pretending to be engaged!' She laughed again, feeling more lighthearted than she had done for days. 'Really, Laurence! If I wanted to come with you, do you think a little thing like gossip would stop me?'

He assumed an offended air. 'It's different for you,' he maintained. 'You're young—and very attractive. And you don't hold any position of authority in the college. I'm its principal. I can't afford to behave in a way that might prove detrimental to my office.'

Caryn relented. 'Oh, Laurence! All right. Don't look so mortified. I know what you mean, but—well, I'll think about it.'

'About what?' He was eager. 'Marrying me?'

'No.' She quickly disabused him. 'Going with you. As your "fiancée", if necessary.'

He leant towards her appealingly. 'Do give it careful thought, won't you?' he implored, but Caryn had the uneasy feeling that her association with Dean Mellor was being stretched to the limits.

It wasn't late when he took her home; no more than ten o'clock. Laurence seldom indulged in late nights. He always said he liked to go to bed and read for an hour before attempting to go to sleep, and consequently he retired earlier to compensate.

Caryn climbed the stairs to her flat rather thoughtfully. She wasn't sure what she ought to do about the trip to America. It was true, the idea of visiting that country was exciting, but as Laurence's fiancée? Real or imagined? She shook her head. Somehow she was loath to commit herself to something that might prove more difficult to get out of later than she could imagine.

There was a light showing under her door, she saw as she reached the top of the stairs, and she frowned. Generally, Laura kept the baby in their flat, finding it easier that way. She did occasionally babysit in Caryn's rooms, but that was usually when Bob was inviting some friends round to play cards, and she had not said anything about that tonight before Caryn went out. Still . . .

Caryn found her key and inserted it in the lock, and entered her living room. Then she stopped in astonishment. Laura was there, sitting nervously on the couch, but opposite her, his long length draped casually over one of Caryn's armchairs, was Tristan Ross.

He came to his feet as she entered, and she noticed half with impatience how incongruous his dark green velvet evening suit looked in the apartment. Before going out she had washed some of the baby's clothes and some nappies, and spread them over a clothes airer to dry. There were some blankets folded over the arm of one chair, and a half empty feeding bottle standing on the table, as well as a pair of her shoes and the tights she had worn for work that day strewn carelessly in one corner.

Laura stood up, too, and looked at her apologetically, making a helpless movement with her shoulders. 'Er—Mr Ross came just after you left, Caryn,' she explained awkwardly. 'He insisted on waiting.'

Caryn pressed her lips together for a moment, and then met Ross's eyes. 'I'm sorry.' She paused. 'You should have phoned.'

He acknowledged this silently, and then looked at Laura.

Taking her cue, she moved clumsily towards the door. But Caryn stopped her: 'Don't go, Laura . . .'

'I think what we have to say needs to be said privately, don't you?' Tristan Ross suggested dryly, almost matching the words she had used at his house, and Laura nodded her head and made for the door.

'He—he's in the bedroom,' she murmured for Caryn's benefit, and Caryn smiled her thanks.

But when the door had closed behind her, Caryn had never felt more humiliated in her life. She despised herself for the slummy state of the room, for the obvious lack of organisation. And she despised him too for coming here and making her feel so small. Was he comparing this place to his beautiful home? How could he not do so? Still, she reflected cynically, perhaps it would persuade him that his child did not deserve to be brought up here.

Now she said curtly: 'Have you seen—him?'

'The boy?' He inclined his head. 'Yes, I've seen him.'

Caryn dropped her handbag on the floor. 'And?'

'He's a beautiful child. You should be proud of him.'

Caryn's lips parted. 'What do you mean?' she demanded.

Tristan Ross thrust his hands into his trousers' pockets, regarding her levelly. Strangely, he seemed unperturbed by his surroundings, and she decided he had no doubt seen worse in East Africa. He was probably prepared for any eventuality, schooled not to show emotion whatever the circumstances. It was his job, after all.

'I mean,' he said, 'that he's obviously been well looked after, whatever your mental aberrations.'

'What mental aberrations?'

He shrugged. 'Loren's death must have been quite a blow,' he reminded her. 'I can appreciate that.'

But she wondered if that was what he had truly meant.

She wanted to ask him what his intentions were, now he had seen the baby. She wanted to ask him if he was prepared to admit that the child was his. But somehow she couldn't fashion the words.

Instead, she walked rather nervously round the room and said: 'Did Laura offer you a drink?'

'Tea, yes. I refused.'

Caryn hesitated. 'I have some sherry . . .'

'I don't want anything,' he replied, glancing significantly at the narrow platinum watch on his wrist. 'I have to leave in less than half an hour. I'm—meeting someone at eleven.'

'Eleven!' Caryn couldn't prevent the ejaculation, and then realised how gauche and provincial she must sound. To someone like him, eleven must seem quite early. But then he didn't have to be up to feed a baby at six-thirty a.m.

Ignoring her interjection, however, he went on: 'I've considered this matter carefully, and subject to certain conditions, I am prepared to support the child.'

'You are!' She stared at him tremblingly, hardly able to believe what he was saying.

'Yes.' He glanced behind him. 'May I sit down?'

'Oh! Oh, yes, of course. Please do.'

'Thank you.' He subsided into the armchair again, sitting with his legs apart, his hands hanging loosely between. He indicated the couch opposite where Laura had been sitting. 'Won't you join me?'

Caryn shook her head. 'I—I'm all right,' she insisted, jerkily, and noticing her agitation, he pulled a wry face.

'I did say—subject to certain conditions,' he murmured. 'I think you ought to sit down while I tell you what those conditions are.'

Caryn came behind the couch, moulding the cushions

under her palms. 'It's all right,' she said, ignoring a sudden twinge of apprehension. 'Go on.'

'Very well.' He looked up at her with those strange amber eyes of his. 'I'll take him to live with me providing you are prepared to come, too. He knows you. And I think he needs you.'

'*What!*' She was glad of the support of the couch now, and she leant against it weakly. 'But I'm no nursemaid!'

'No, you're a secretary. You work for the Dean of Lansworth College, a man called Laurence Mellor. The man you've been dining with this evening, according to your friend Mrs Weston.'

'How do you—have you had me investigated?' She was aghast.

'I have a very efficient office. It's their job to find out about people. Particularly people I have to interview.'

'But I'm not one of your—your television interviewees!'

'No,' he conceded evenly. 'But I had to check your story, didn't I?'

'And—Loren . . .'

'And Loren,' he agreed.

Her lips curled. 'How cold-blooded can you get!'

'Practical,' he retorted calmly. 'Now, shall we discuss the details——'

'I wouldn't work for you!' She glared angrily at him. 'And you forget, I have a job!'

'I haven't forgotten anything. At least, I think not. The summer vacation starts in a matter of two weeks. By the time September comes round I'm sure Dean Mellor can find himself another secretary.'

'You're forgetting the fact that I wouldn't live in your house if you paid me in diamonds!' she stormed.

He shrugged. 'Then the deal's off.'

'What do you mean?'

'Exactly what I say.'

'But you've admitted—the child's yours——'

'I've admitted nothing!' he told her curtly. 'I said I was prepared to bring him up with certain conditions satisfied. If you're not prepared to satisfy those conditions, then I wash my hands of the whole affair.'

Caryn put a confused hand to her head, brushing back the moist hair at her temple. 'You can't do this . . .'

'Why not?'

She thought desperately. 'I—I'll go to the papers . . .'

'What will you say? How will you prove your allegations?'

'Loren was your secretary when she became pregnant.'

'So what? If every employer was blamed when their secretaries became pregnant . . .'

'You—you swine!'

'Why? Because I tell the truth. Who would believe you?'

'Mud sticks.'

'All right.' He rose to his feet. 'So you ruin me. What good does that do you?'

Caryn's lips trembled. 'I'll do it.'

'I can't stop you.' He walked towards the door. 'I'll bid you goodnight, then——'

'No!' Her cry was agonised. 'Mr Ross, please! How can you deny your own son?'

'How can you deny your nephew? He is your sister's flesh and blood, isn't he?'

Caryn faltered. 'What would I be expected to do?'

'Well, I'm not asking you to be his nursemaid.'

'But—you said——'

'I said he needed you. I think he does. But I'm prepared to employ a nanny to take care of his physical needs.'

Caryn looked blank. 'Then—what should I do?'

He paused by the door. 'I need a secretary. I have it on good authority that you're very efficient——' his eyes flickered sardonically round the room, '—in that direction.'

Caryn's face flamed. 'I intended to tidy up before you came,' she exclaimed defensively, and a faint smile lifted the corners of his mouth.

'I believe you. Well? Does this make a difference?' He looked at his watch again. 'I don't have much time.'

'But you can't expect me to decide a thing like this on the spur of the moment . . .'

'Why not?' He was unsympathetic. 'You know now what you really feel.'

Caryn glanced unwillingly towards the closed bedroom door. She had wanted *him* out of her life for good. Everything she had done for him she had done coolly and clinically, refusing to allow him to wind his way into her heart. She had known that sooner or later someone would come along and take him away from her, that she simply couldn't care for him alone. Now Tristan Ross was making her acknowledge him as an individual, as her nephew, asking her to witness his development, forging a bond of time between them that would inevitably become impossible to break.

She turned back to him, her face composed, only her eyes revealing the torment she was suffering. 'Very well,' she said dully, 'I'll do it.'

'Good.' She had the feeling he had known all along that she would submit. But then he was used to dealing with people; he knew exactly the right line to take to achieve his own ends. 'When can you be ready to leave?'

Caryn caught her lower lip between her teeth. 'As—as you

pointed out, the summer vacation begins in a couple of weeks . . .'

Belatedly, she remembered Laurence's trip to America. At least that was that particular problem solved. But what was she going to tell him?

'So you'll come as soon as the college closes,' Tristan Ross was saying, and reluctantly she nodded.

'I—I shall have to give notice.'

'To Mellor. I know.' Tristan frowned. 'What will you say?'

Caryn shook her head. 'I don't know . . .'

'I suggest you tell him you saw an advertisement for a secretary in South Wales, and when you applied I permitted you to bring the child along. Naturally, you didn't know it was me at the time of the application.'

'I did ask for time off to visit a sick relative in Wales,' she murmured, half to himself.

'There you are, then.' His expression was wry. 'You can tell him I remembered Loren, if you like.'

'But . . .' Caryn looked anxiously at him. 'Won't that look rather—odd?'

'Mellor doesn't move in the same circles I do. Why should it look odd? It's a generous gesture, that's all.'

'Generous!' Caryn sounded bitter, and his brows quirked.

'It is, believe me,' he assured her. 'You'll find out, one of these days.'

He swung open the door, and suddenly she realised exactly what she was committing herself to. 'I—I don't know what a secretary of yours would do,' she exclaimed, and he gave her a humorous look.

'Take shorthand, answer letters, file papers; I presume you can do all those things.'

Caryn nodded stiffly. 'Of course.'

'Problem solved. I'll be in touch about the nursemaid.'

'You'll be in touch?' She didn't understand what he meant.

'I thought you might prefer to choose a nanny. I don't know much about these things.'

Caryn was taken aback, but she had other things on her mind. 'Mr Ross . . . your daughter . . .'

'Leave Angel to me,' he retorted shortly, and with a brief salute, he left her.

CHAPTER FOUR

It was early evening when the waters of the estuary came into view, and feeling the refreshing breeze that drifted off them, Caryn breathed a silent sigh of relief. It had been a long hot afternoon, and the humidity of the weather had contributed to the baby's discomfort. He had cried intermittently since leaving Gloucester, and she was inordinately glad she had Miss Trewen with her. Without the nanny's assistance, the journey would have seemed interminable, and she supposed she ought to feel grateful to Tristan Ross for suggesting they drove down together. Miss Trewen came from a famous nursing agency which prided itself on the competence of its members, and her previous employers had recommended her highly. That they had also held an aristocratic title meant less than the warmth in which they had held her, and Miss Trewen herself had confided that she had been with them for more than fifteen years. Caryn was rather bemused by the arrangement, never having had to deal with staff of any kind before, but as with everything else, Miss Trewen was more than up to handling the situation. Her age, like everything else about her, was indeterminate, but her gentleness and compassion were more than evident.

It seemed more than three weeks since she had last made this journey, Caryn reflected, but it wasn't. Yet so much had happened. So much had changed. And remembering her final interview with Laurence Mellor she was almost glad she was leaving London.

He had been shocked, of course, as she had known he

would be. What she had not been prepared for was his jealous resentment.

'I thought I could trust you, Caryn,' he had said coldly, and when she protested that he could, he went on: 'You led me to believe you were as eager as I was for you to be free of the child. Now you say you're keeping him! Do the social services know about this?'

'Oh, Laurence!' Caryn sighed. 'Surely you could try and understand. Until now, there's been no question of me—well, keeping him. But if—if Mr Ross has no objections . . .'

'Tristan Ross!' Laurence sounded disgusted. 'I thought you said he fired Loren. What's he doing hiring you?'

Caryn flushed at this. 'Perhaps I'm better at my job.'

'And did you know whose secretary you were going to be when you went for this interview?'

'No. I've told you.' Caryn crossed her fingers. 'I—answered an advertisement.'

'And you lied to me,' he reminded her. 'A sick relative! Oh, Caryn, how could you?'

'I—thought a change might do us—both good.'

'And you knew this when I took you out for dinner? When I asked you to marry me? You let me go on hoping . . .'

'Laurence, I hadn't got the job then.'

'But you knew there was a possibility.'

'Oh—all right. Yes.' She sighed. 'Laurence, I could never have gone to the States with you. I know that.'

'Why?'

'Oh, because—because our relationship is getting too—too intense.'

'I don't agree with you. I think we work very well together. Now, after the holidays are over I shall have all the unpleasantness of educating a new girl into my ways.'

'Laurence!' She felt worse than ever. 'Please don't take it this way. I'd like us to—to remain friends.'

But he had maintained an aloofness towards her for the re-remainder of the college term, and only on her last afternoon did he relent sufficiently to shake her hand and wish her luck in rather gruff emotional tones. Caryn had been astonished. She had never realised what an emotional man he could be, and she wondered with a pang whether she ought not to have accepted his proposal after all. Maybe if he had been prepared to take the child as well . . .

It was too late now. That particular stage of her life was over, and her only regret was at leaving Laura and Bob. She knew Laura would miss the baby terribly, but in another ten weeks or so she would have a baby of her own, and then he would soon be forgotten. Because she had not known how long she was to stay in Wales, reluctantly she had had to let the flat go, too. But she couldn't afford to pay rent when she was not living there, and as yet she had no real idea of what financial arrangements Tristan Ross was going to make. He was already paying for the nanny. Would he expect her to support herself? Perhaps by working for him she would simply be allaying the expense.

'Is it much further, Miss Stevens?'

Miss Trewen was speaking to her from the back of the small saloon, and Caryn glanced over her shoulder. 'About half a mile,' she assured the older woman. 'I hope he's not been too much of a nuisance to you.'

'Heavens, no.' Miss Trewen sounded quite shocked. 'But we are wanting our supper.'

It took Caryn a moment to realise she meant that the baby was wanting his supper, and she hid a rueful smile. The royal 'we'. She would have to remember that.

The road crossed the suspension bridge and descended

towards Druid's Fleet. The salty tang of the air was invigorating, and Caryn breathed deeply. There were going to be advantages to living here, there was no doubt about that. Whether they would compensate for the position Tristan Ross was putting her in remained to be seen.

She heard the sound of the music before they reached the gates of the drive. This time she turned between the gates, and let the small Renault coast the final few yards down to the house. It was a beautiful July evening and every window in the house seemed to be open emitting the deafening sound of beat music emanating from the kind of instruments Caryn had hitherto only heard in the Albert Hall. Miss Trewen tapped her shoulder, looking most concerned.

'What is that?'

Caryn was wondering the same thing herself. 'I don't know,' she admitted apologetically. Was Tristan Ross giving a party? she speculated anxiously. He knew they were expected this afternoon. Surely he realised this kind of atmosphere was not suitable for a baby—not, at least, until he was used to his new surroundings. And as for Miss Trewen ... Caryn shook her head. The nanny was looking distinctly troubled.

It didn't help when the baby awoke at that moment and chose to add his own cacophony to the din. Bidding Miss Trewen to remain where she was for the moment, Caryn thrust open her door and got out. Wherever Tristan Ross was, she would find him, and when she did ...

Slim and aggressive in her cream denims and cotton vest, she marched round to the door only to find it standing wide, like the windows.

'Mr Ross?'

Her words were drowned in the wave of sound that seemed to be coming from the back of the house. Gritting her teeth, she stepped into the upper hall and called again. Again there was no answer, and with a heavy sigh she descended the stairs to the lower level.

The noise was louder here, and she began to realise that what she could hear was actually instruments, not merely records, as she had surmised at first. Who on earth was it? And what was going on?

The sound led her across the hall to the door through which the housekeeper, Marcia, had passed the evening Caryn had first come to the house. She had thought it only led to the kitchens, but perhaps she was wrong.

With a definite feeling of trespass, she opened the door and went through. She could hear voices now, as well as the music, and laughter. Her fists balled. It was a party, then. What on earth did he think he was doing?

Beyond the door, the passage ran towards a huge glass-roofed loggia, and it was from here the noise was coming. As she made her way along the passage, Caryn began to glimpse young people moving among banks of greenery, their bodies undulating in time to the music. There was the smell of tobacco and alcohol, and the faint sweet aroma of joss sticks, and Caryn had no doubt now that it was a party. But whose? And for whom?

As she hesitated outside the loggia, a young man saw her and with admiring appraisal spreading over his face came towards her. 'Well, hello!' he greeted her warmly. 'Who are you? I don't remember seeing you at one of Angel's parties before.'

Angel! Caryn might have known. But where was Tristan Ross?

'I'm—not at the party,' she explained now, stepping into the loggia to put some space between them, and looking about her impatiently. There must have been about thirty

people there, either talking or dancing or watching
the group of musicians on a small dais at the far end of the
verandah. None of them was paying any attention to the
view which, like the sitting room above, overlooked the
estuary, and nobody seemed to notice her either, dressed as
she was in the kind of clothes they were all wearing. A table
supporting an assortment of bottles was strewn with dirty
glasses, and the air was getting quite thick with cigarette
smoke.

'You're not at the party?' The young man was right
behind her. 'It sure looks that way to me.'

Caryn sighed, and turned to him. 'Where is Mr Ross?'

'Who?'

'Mr Ross. Tristan Ross. Angel—Angela Ross's father.'

'Oh, Angel's daddy!' He nodded his head slowly, pulling
out a pack of cigarettes and offering her one. Caryn refused,
and he put one between his lips before continuing: 'He's not
here.' He lit the cigarette and grinned. 'But you're here, and
I'm here. So how about we get it together, hmm?'

Caryn gave him a crippling look. 'Just tell me where
—Angela is,' she said coldly.

'Come on! Do you know who that is over there?'

'I don't particularly care——'

'That's Sweet Vibration, honey. Now don't tell me you
haven't heard of them.'

Caryn blinked and looked again at the group on the dais.
She had heard of Sweet Vibration, of course she had. Their
last record had been Number One on the best-seller charts
for five weeks, and in spite of her annoyance she was
impressed. She supposed that was what came of having
someone like Tristan Ross for a father. But that still didn't
alter the fact that he had known they were arriving this
afternoon, and had absented himself so his daughter could

throw the kind of party designed to unnerve the most patient of nursemaids.

'Just tell me where Angela is,' Caryn repeated now, and somewhat offended, the young man indicated a group of people gathered near the dais.

'Right on,' he drawled, and wincing at his Americanism, Caryn began to make her way towards the other girl.

It wasn't easy. Several of the young men swung her round, obviously imagining she was some late arrival, and she was feeling the heat and lack of air by the time she reached Angela Ross's circle. It didn't help when Tristan's daughter regarded her without evident recognition.

'Yes?' she said, and in that moment Caryn knew Angela knew exactly who she was.

'I'm looking for your father,' Caryn told her, refusing to be intimidated. 'Perhaps you could tell me when he'll be back.'

Angel shrugged, and the group of boys and girls around her exchanged amused glances. 'Why do you want him?' she asked.

Caryn was tempted to tell her, right there in front of her friends. She wondered how Angela would feel if she announced that she had brought her father's illegitimate son to live with them. How much did the girl know? How much had he chosen to tell her?

'Just tell me when he'll be back,' she said, impaling the younger girl with her green gaze, and Angela unwillingly relented.

'I don't know,' she retorted shortly. 'I don't keep tabs on him.'

Caryn controlled her temper. 'Well, is there some way I can get in touch with him?'

Angela pouted. 'You can ring the studios, if you like. But he won't like it.'

'Thank you.'

Caryn was turning away when a hand descended on her shoulder, and she swung round aggressively to find a boy behind her whose face was curiously familiar. Then she realised. He was Dave O'Hara, the lead guitarist with Sweet Vibration. Her senses quivered pleasurably, and she was unable to summon the anger she had felt a moment before when she had thought the man who had met her was touching her.

'Is something wrong?'

Dave O'Hara's voice was definitely Liverpudlian in origin, overlaid with a veneer that combined a southern drawl with a transatlantic nasalism. But it was a friendly voice, and when Caryn looked at him, his eyes were friendly, too. He wasn't a lot taller than she was, and stockily built, with the short cut hair that was peculiar to their image.

'Nothing's wrong, Dave,' Angela said now, asserting herself. 'My father's new secretary's arrived, that's all. Inconveniently, as usual.'

Dave ignored Angela and continued to look at Caryn, his hand continuing to rest on her shoulder. 'Is that right?' he said. 'You're going to work for Tris?'

Caryn nodded. 'I was just looking for him.'

'Oh, hey, he'll be along in a minute,' Dave assured her. 'He was called away rather unexpectedly, isn't that right, Angel?'

Now he looked at the other girl and she moved her shoulders in an indifferent gesture. In tight-fitting jeans and a flowing chiffon smock, Angela adopted a seductive air, but the young guitarist looked right through her.

'I know what I'm talking about,' he maintained, turning

back to Caryn. 'Tris lets us rehearse here sometimes, and when we do Angel usually hauls in a gang of her cronies to join the party. When Tris was called away this afternoon, Angel called me. Enough said?'

It explained a lot, and Caryn was grateful. 'I'm sorry if I've spoiled the party,' she apologised.

'Are you?' Angela was still aggressive. 'I'll get Marcia to show you to your room.'

'Now is that any way to treat a guest?' Dave protested, at once, and she grimaced.

'Miss Stevens is not a guest!' she retorted, and then bit her lip when Dave's eyes narrowed at the use of Caryn's name.

'Miss Stevens!' he echoed. 'Say, that's a coincidence.'

'No, it's not,' declared Angela shortly. 'She's Loren's sister.'

'Is that so?' Dave looked at Caryn again. 'Well, what do you know?'

Caryn's brows drew together. 'You knew my sister?'

'Everyone knew your sister,' retorted Angela dryly. 'Didn't you know?'

Caryn coloured, but before she could make any retaliatory response, an angry masculine voice broke into the proceedings. It was a voice Caryn recognised only too well, and as if in sympathy the musicians still on the dais dissolved into discord and finally silence.

'I asked what the hell is going on here?' Tristan Ross stalked across the room towards them, and Caryn noticed that even Dave's hand fell from her shoulder. 'Angel! For heaven's sake, have you taken leave of your senses?'

Angela looked sulky. 'I don't know what all the panic's about——' she began, but her father interrupted her.

'I told you Miss Stevens and the child were arriving this afternoon!' he stated coldly. 'And what do I find? A red-faced nursemaid sitting indignantly in a car at the door trying to comfort a screaming child, while the most God-awful din is going on in here!' His gaze flickered almost malevolently over Caryn. 'What have you been doing? Succumbing to the Sweet Vibrations?'

'No!' Caryn was indignant, too.

'That's right.' Dave joined in. 'She came looking for you, Tris. And,' he added humorously, 'I don't dig being called a God-awful din!'

Tristan ignored that. 'I've installed Miss Trewen and her charge in the sitting room for the moment, but I want you lot out of here in five minutes, understand?' He faced his daughter. 'And the next time you do something like this, you'll join them.'

Angela pulled a face at him and turned away, as Tristan's hand came beneath Caryn's elbow. 'Come with me,' he said. 'I want to reassure Miss Trewen you haven't been swallowed up in the mêlée.'

Caryn went with him almost gratefully. In spite of Dave O'Hara's kindness, the noise and confusion had been unnerving for someone who had just driven over two hundred miles, and now the silence was almost as deafening.

He released her as they reached the door into the passage and she went ahead of him towards the second door and through it into the lower hall. The door to the sitting room was closed, but when she would have crossed to it, he stopped her.

'Any problems?' he asked, and although Caryn shook herself free of his hand she paused to answer him.

He had obviously come straight from the studio, and was still wearing the formal attire of a mohair lounge suit and matching waistcoat. She could well imagine an impressionable girl like Loren comparing his cool sophistication with the wilder elements Caryn herself had just encountered and finding them lacking . . .

'No,' she said now, realising he was waiting for her reply. 'What problems could there be?'

'You approve of Miss Trewen, then?' he enquired, in a low tone, and she nodded half in embarrassment.

'How could I not? She's very efficient. You read her references too, didn't you?'

'References are not everything,' he stated flatly. 'I should know that.'

Caryn shrugged. 'You must know I've had no experience in dealing with—with employees, of any kind.'

'But you like her,' he insisted.

'Yes.'

'Good.' He frowned, gesturing behind him. 'I'm sorry about this—affair. Angel didn't take too kindly to the idea of having a baby in the house, and I guess she was just making her point.'

Caryn shifted uncomfortably. 'I can believe it.'

He sighed. 'I've told her the child is your nephew.'

'Is that all?' Caryn gasped.

His expression hardened. 'What else is there?'

She gulped. 'You ask me that!'

He looked impatient now. 'Look, this is neither the time nor the place to start those sort of arguments. I'm prepared to give you and the child a home. For the moment that should be enough.'

'Well, it's not,' she stormed angrily. 'What is—*she* going to think I am?'

'Who? Miss Trewen?' He shrugged. 'She knows——'

'Not Miss Trewen! Angela!'

'Did someone call me?' Angela herself floated into the hall at that moment followed by an assortment of young people and musicians, some carrying instruments, some not.

Tristan turned to her impatiently. 'I see you're moving out. Not a moment too soon.'

'See you!' called Dave O'Hara to Caryn as he went by, and Caryn couldn't suppress an answering smile.

Tristan intercepted their greeting and indicated the sitting room. 'I suggest we move before we're trampled underfoot,' he asserted shortly, and Caryn had perforce to go with him.

Miss Trewen was pacing the floor with the baby in her arms. She looked much relieved to see Caryn, and the girl felt a moment's sympathy for her. This must be much different from the circumstances she was used to. But Tristan Ross seemed in no way perturbed.

'I suppose you think this is a madhouse!' he declared, bestowing upon her the smile that had won him so many admirers. 'I have to apologise for the reception. Obviously I didn't make the position clear and my daughter chose this evening to invite her friends round.'

He could be charm itself when he chose, Caryn thought rather maliciously, wishing Miss Trewen would tell him exactly what she had thought of the fiasco. But the elderly nanny was easily placated.

'Our young man is hungry,' she explained, with a smile. 'And it's been a long drive. Do you think you could show me the nursery, and then I can attend to his needs?'

'Of course.' Tristan nodded at once, going to the door and shouting: 'Marcia, will you come here?'

It wasn't difficult to attract the housekeeper's attention now that the house was quiet again. Marcia appeared, tall and attractive as usual, in a cerise overall this time. She looked questioningly towards Caryn and Miss Trewen, her face softening as her eyes rested on the child, and then turned politely to Tristan.

'I want you to show Miss Stevens and Miss Trewen to their rooms,' he said, and she nodded. Then he looked at the elderly nursemaid. 'Marcia is dumb,' he explained quietly. 'But if necessary, she can converse in sign language or on paper.'

Miss Trewen looked shocked but managed to silence any comment she might have been tempted to make, but Marcia surprised them all by going across to her and laying gentle fingers on the baby's head. Her face took on such an expression of gentleness that Caryn felt a lump come into her throat, and she looked at Tristan almost compulsively. He, of all of them, seemed the least surprised, and after a moment he said: 'Marcia!' again, in compelling tones, and with a faint smile she nodded her head and indicated that they should follow her.

'The cases...' murmured Caryn, as Miss Trewen followed the housekeeper, but Tristan shook his head.

'I'll fetch them,' he said. 'Where are your keys?'

'In the ignition,' Caryn admitted reluctantly. 'But I could get them.'

His smile was wry. 'Believe it or not, but I am capable of carrying a couple of suitcases.'

'There's more than a couple,' Caryn protested, remembering the roof-rack. 'And the pram, and the cot...'

'I'll get help, don't worry,' he assured her, and rather unwillingly she hurried after the others.

Marcia led the way up the stairs to the entrance hall, and from there, up a second flight of stairs to the upper floor. Caryn would not have liked to guess how many levels the house occupied. There were four she knew of, and even above them, a wooden ladder led to the loft.

But the upper floor was spacious, gracefully dividing into two wings with a central gallery that overlooked the lower halls. Arched doorways led into the individual wings of the house, with long corridors lined with white panelled doors. Miss Trewen was obviously impressed with the appointments of the building, and Caryn could hardly blame her.

A softly-piled cream carpet led them into the south wing, and Marcia traversed the full length of the corridor before halting outside a door at the end. She threw it wide, and they entered into a light sunny apartment, with windows on two sides, and walls decorated with characters from Winnie the Pooh and Peter Rabbit to Paddington Bear and the Wombles. The long windows which overlooked the cliffs and the estuary had been reinforced with safety bars along the lower panes, and as well as an assortment of toys which would have delighted any toddler, there was a pint-sized table and chairs, also decorated with transfers, and a rocker that Miss Trewen at once claimed for her own.

In one corner of the nursery there was a small electric hotplate, an electric kettle, and a sink, together with a cupboard which, when Marcia opened it, was shown to contain all the necessary equipment for feeding a baby. It was very comprehensive, and Caryn glanced rather apprehensively at the nurse.

While she was taking in the fact that someone had taken a great deal of trouble to make everything attractive, Marcia went ahead and opened the door into an adjoining room. Here a blue-painted cot, and a pile of bed-linen sitting on a cushion-topped ottoman, indicated that this was where the child was intended to sleep, and Caryn felt her face turning redder by the minute.

Miss Trewen, however, looked a little perturbed. 'Didn't Mr Ross know you were fetching your own cot and feeding bottles?' she asked, hushing the baby as he started to whimper again.

'Apparently not.' Caryn glanced awkwardly at Marcia. 'Thank you.'

Marcia permitted herself a slight smile. It was the first communication she had acknowledged between them and Caryn felt a moment's relief before feeling again the discomfort of the situation. How could she maintain the fiction of only being an employee when Tristan Ross treated her like this? Soon Miss Trewen was going to suspect the child was hers—hers and Tristan Ross's!

Meanwhile, Marcia was continuing with the tour. She was apparently enjoying herself, and Caryn trailed behind them. Beyond the child's bedroom was a room allotted to Miss Trewen, with a bathroom between.

Caryn wondered where she was to sleep. Surely not with Miss Trewen, although the nurse's room did contain two beds. But before they went any further, Tristan Ross appeared in the doorway to the nursery, two suitcases in one hand and one in the other. Behind him came an elderly man carrying Miss Trewen's belongings, and the picnic hamper in which Caryn had packed all the baby's feeding equipment.

'Well?' Tristan set down the cases outside the door with some relief, and walked into the room. 'Is everything satisfactory?'

Caryn gave him an exasperated look. 'More than satisfactory,' she declared shortly, and his eyes flickered mockingly.

'Marcia had a free hand in equipping the place,' he remarked, his eyes resting on the child for a moment. Then he looked at Caryn. 'Don't you approve?'

Miss Trewen interposed then. 'Of course we do, Mr Ross,' she exclaimed, 'but it's most unusual for everything to be provided like this, down to the last detail.'

Tristan shrugged. 'Blame Marcia.'

'I don't blame anyone,' she protested, looking a trifle flustered herself now. 'I'm sure Miss—er—Stevens is quite—overcome.'

'Are you overcome, Miss Stevens?' he mocked, and Caryn had to bite her tongue to prevent the ready retort from bursting from her.

'Where am I to sleep?' she asked instead, deliberately keeping all expression out of her voice, and he raised his eyebrows at the housekeeper.

'Haven't you shown Miss Stevens her room?' he asked, and when Marcia shook her head, he added: 'Allow me!'

He was making fun of her, but short of being rude to him there was nothing she could say. He indicated to the elderly man to leave the nurse's cases in the nursery, and then invited Caryn to follow him. They went a few yards along the corridor before he opened a door and ushered her, protesting, into a large, comfortable bed-sitting room. That he also closed the door behind him in no way relieved the tension she was feeling, and ignoring the exquisite green and gold appointments of the apartment she turned to him angrily.

'Are you mad?' she demanded.

'Mad?' He lifted his shoulders indifferently. 'Perhaps. You obviously think so.'

Caryn seethed. 'You do realise what you've done, don't you?'

He pretended to consider the matter. 'You think I don't?'

'Stop anticipating me!' she exclaimed frustratedly. 'You are aware you've made Miss Trewen suspicious, aren't you?'

'Suspicious?'

'Yes, suspicious!' Caryn sighed, trying not to be disconcerted by the unexpected indulgence of his regard. 'What employer would provide a nursery like—like that, for the use of—of the nephew of one of his employees——'

'Wait a minute,' he interrupted her. 'Didn't you just complain that I wasn't making sufficient provision for you downstairs?'

Caryn glared at him. 'That was different . . .'

'Oh?'

'I thought you ought to have told your daughter the truth.'

'What makes you so sure I haven't?'

'You always answer with a question, don't you?' she sniffed. 'The fact remains, Miss Trewen thought it odd——'

'I don't give a damn what Miss Trewen thinks,' he told her succinctly, flexing his shoulder muscles, unconsciously drawing Caryn's attention to the dark skin of his chest shadowed beneath the cream silk of his shirt. 'Does that satisfy you?'

Caryn shifted uneasily. 'What do you mean?'

'I mean Miss Trewen is an employee, just as you are, and she'll take her orders from me or get out! Right?'

His ruthlessness was all the more disturbing after his earlier tolerance and Caryn realised anew that so far as she was concerned he was completely unpredictable.

'Yes, *sir*!' she responded now, and had the gratification of seeing her words hit the mark.

'There's no need to be insolent,' he said sharply, and she held up her head.

'If you'll just explain to me my position here, I won't say another word,' she retorted, and he pushed back the weight of his hair with an impatient hand.

'What now?'

'Miss Trewen thinks she's my employee,' Caryn related with scarcely-veiled sarcasm. 'Perhaps you could explain the position to her.'

The oath he stifled was unrepeatable, and Caryn's fingers sought the back hip pockets of her jeans as she shifted uncomfortably before him.

'Are you afraid she'll think the child's yours?' he demanded, and she gave an offhand shrug. 'Because if you are I'm afraid you're going to have to live with it. I see no reason to supply a nursemaid with the personal details of our life here.'

'And if she thinks the child's yours, too?' Caryn suggested provokingly, and his lips twisted.

'That's her prerogative. Yours, too, as it happens.'

'He is your son!'

'I see you still persist in avoiding his name. I assume he has been registered.'

'Of course.'

'In my name?'

Caryn bent her head. 'No.'

'No?'

She looked up. 'The priest—the one who attended Loren at the end—he registered the child.'

'And?'

'He put it that the father was unknown.'

'My God!' He gave a low whistle. 'And the name?'

'I told you, Loren called him Tristan.'

'And he was registered as Tristan?'

'Yes.'

'So!' He frowned. 'Two Tristans. That won't do.'

'I don't see why not. I shall call you Mr Ross. So, I presume, will Miss Trewen.'

'And Tristan?' Caryn frowned her incomprehension, and he prompted: 'Junior! The baby! What will he call me?'

Caryn couldn't resist it: 'Daddy?' she suggested, and saw his sudden anger.

'He's not my son,' he declared shortly. 'I should have thought you'd have realised that by now.'

'Why? Why should I? Why should you have us here otherwise?'

'Christian charity?' he suggested dryly, and then shook his head. 'Oh, let's not start that particular argument again right now. It looks like we'll have to call him Tristan for the time being. Fortunately Angel calls me Tris, which does make a distinction.'

'Why doesn't she call you her father?' asked Caryn impulsively, and he regarded her sardonically.

'I suppose you're thinking I'm too vain to admit to having a daughter of nineteen, is that it?'

Caryn flushed, but she forced herself to go on: 'Are you?'

'Calling me Tris was Angel's idea. Around the studios it's easier, for one thing, and she prefers it. Does that answer your question?'

'It's nothing to do with me really.'

'I'd go along with that. However, I find it easier to put the record straight at the beginning.'

Caryn suddenly realised how long they had been standing here, in her bedroom, talking. If Miss Trewen had been suspicious before, what must she be thinking now?

'I think you ought to go,' she said abruptly, and saw his dawning indignation.

'You think what?' he demanded.

'Miss Trewen must be wondering what we're doing. You shouldn't have closed the door.'

'No? You'd have liked Marcia and the nanny to hear all our conversation?'

'No, but . . .' She sighed once more. 'I suppose I should thank you. For—for what you've done. But——'

'—you find it hard?' His mouth turned down at the

corners and he reached for the handle of the door. 'Don't fret about it. I can do without your gratitude. Dinner is at eight. Do you think you can find your way downstairs by then?'

'Oh, but——' Caryn broke off awkwardly. Then: 'Will Miss Trewen be eating downstairs?'

'I imagine Miss Trewen will take all her meals in the nursery,' he essayed, swinging open the door. 'But don't be alarmed. I shan't be joining you for the meal. I have a dinner engagement already—one I shouldn't care to miss.'

And with a mocking smile, he left her.

CHAPTER FIVE

It was possible to reach the village across the mud-flats at low tide. Then the sandy bottom of the river was criss-crossed with the claw-marks of half a dozen different sea birds, all of whom came to feed on the seaweed and other debris left stranded by the tide. As it was holiday time, the birds had to take their chance with the children who scrambled down the cliffs to the beaches that lay beneath them, and the dozens of small craft that bobbed about like corks when the tide came in. Port Edward was not a holiday resort exactly, but its charm and beauty attracted a great number of visitors, whose cars jammed the narrow streets and made the locals grumble that they couldn't get about their daily business.

Druid's Fleet was remote from the hustle and bustle of the village. Caryn had soon learned that the steps which descended from the house to the waterline led not to the river, but a small creek which ran into it. Here, amid a thickly planted screen of trees, Tristan Ross had his boathouse, and although she had not been aboard the craft, she had glimpsed its sleek lines through the boathouse windows. She learned that Druid's Fleet was actually the name of the creek, fleet being a word of German origin meaning small stream or inlet, and that when Tristan bought this house it had indeed been called Water's Reach.

She learned this from Pepper, the gardener and general factotum, the elderly man who had helped Tristan carry up their cases that first day. Pepper had lived in Port Edward all his life, and he was steeped in the history of the place. He resembled its first early settlers, those exiles of Mediterranean origin, with short stocky bodies and dark features, whose

73

curious megaliths rear their stone heads throughout the western area of Britain, but he had all the love of language of his Welsh ancestry. In those first days at Druid's Fleet he seemed Caryn's only friend, surrounded as she was by Marcia's silence, Angela's hostility, and Tristan Ross's enigmatism.

The child settled down well in his new surroundings, as well he might, thought Caryn rather uncharitably. A flat in London, constantly within sight and sound of people and traffic, could not compare with the peace and tranquillity of the Levant estuary, and with Miss Trewen's constant attention he thrived vigorously.

Miss Trewen herself adjusted, chameleon-like, to the change of scene. Somehow, she and Marcia managed to achieve a kind of communication, and their mutual affection for the young Tristan was a more than adequate reason for their liking for one another.

Angela, for her part, made no effort to adjust. Her obvious resentment that having a child in the house curtailed the amount of freedom she had for inviting people there was understandable, but Caryn, remembering her sister, could not help but think she was selfish. However, the younger girl departed with some friends for a holiday in Barbados only a week after their arrival, which relieved the situation somewhat.

Working for Tristan Ross, Caryn found, was not like working for Laurence Mellor. To begin with, Tristan was seldom about when she was working, and seemed to prefer to leave all his instructions on the dictaphone for her to deal with while he was away. She had wondered how she would fill her time, used as she was to the régime of an office, but her fears of being idle proved groundless.

There was an amazing amount of correspondence to deal

with, for one thing. Every letter, no matter how ingratiating or conversely how disgusting, had to be read, and replies had to be drafted. Caryn got into the habit of leaving those letters which required his personal attention to one side, and answered those that didn't herself. Every letter she wrote was left for his perusal, and very often she would go down to his study in the morning early to find him having already put in at least a couple of hours' work. Only occasionally did he work in the study when she did, and then it was mostly making telephone calls arranging interviews with people, or alternatively making apologetic refusals to some of the dozens of invitations he got to attend local functions. But his main work concerned his television appearances, and it was this which occupied most of Caryn's time. At the moment, he was contracted to make a series of programmes concerning the economy for a London television company, and in consequence he spent a lot of time visiting factories around the country, speaking to workers and management alike.

Surprisingly, Caryn enjoyed her work. Perhaps it was that in those early days she kept very much to herself, and what free time she had after the baby was in bed, she spent exploring her surroundings. She tried to spend at least an hour each evening in the nursery while Miss Trewen ate her supper in peace, and then, because it was less daunting, she ate her own meal in her room. She did offer to babysit, but the nurse refused the opportunity to go out.

'I'm not much of a one for going places,' she told Caryn ruefully. 'I never have been.'

'But you must have some time off,' Caryn protested, making a mental note to mention this to Tristan next time she saw him. 'What day would suit you best?'

Miss Trewen shook her head. 'I've already spoken to Mr Ross,' she explained, surprising the girl. 'I explained how it

was when I worked for the Tranters. I preferred to save my
days off until I could take a proper break.'

'I see.'

Caryn had no choice but to accept this. Even so, she
thought resentfully that it was typical of Tristan Ross's attitude not to mention it to her.

Her opportunity to make her feelings felt came sooner
than she expected. The following morning she found him
waiting for her when she entered the study after breakfast,
and judging from his appearance he was on the point of
leaving.

'I've left a draft of the first programme on the tape,' he
said at once, after bidding her a curt good morning. He was
usually curt in the mornings, and Caryn had assumed he was
one of those people who didn't like getting up. But for once
she detained him when he would have departed.

'Mr Ross . . .'

'Yes?' He was clearly impatient, but she refused to be
hustled.

'I understand Miss Trewen contacted you about her time
off.'

He sighed, fastening the button of his leather jacket.
'That's right, she did,' he conceded, nodding. 'So? The
woman wants to take a week, or maybe two weeks at a
stretch. You have no objections, do you?'

Caryn caught her breath. 'It would be all the same if I
had.'

His mouth turned down at the corners. 'What is it? I'm
sure Marcia will be only too willing to share the nursing
duties with you when it becomes necessary, if that's
what——'

'That's not the point! You should have told me.'

'So—I forgot. No sweat!'

Caryn squared her shoulders. 'You persist in taking matters over my head——'

'Oh, come on!' He was losing the battle with his temper, and it was beginning to show. 'You've been here—how long? A week? How often have we conversed in that time?'

'You're seldom at home . . .'

'And when I am, you eat in your room.'

'That's not fair. We see each other in working hours.'

'Look, right now I'm involved in this economy thing. When I talk to my secretary, I talk to my secretary, not to young Tristan's aunt! Now, if you have any complaints to make, you save them for your time, not mine!'

Caryn gasped. She had forgotten how harsh his tongue could be. 'Yes, Mr Ross,' she responded tautly, her chin quivering, and with a stifled curse he left her.

For the rest of that day, Caryn worked harder than she had ever done before. She didn't know whether his comments had been a criticism or otherwise, but she determined he should have no complaints to make about her work. By tea time her eyes were aching, and when Marcia brought her tray she looked concerned when she saw Caryn's pale face. She usually brought her tea to the study, but today after setting down the tray, she pointed at the girl and then placed her forefingers at the corners of her eyes and pushed the skin of her cheekbones back expressively.

Caryn was moved by the sympathetic demonstration and nodded wearily. 'Yes, I'm tired,' she admitted, pushing the typewriter to one side. She pulled the tray towards her. 'Mmm, I'm going to enjoy this.'

Marcia hesitated. Although her attitude to Caryn had not altered, having a baby in the house had definitely softened her nature. Pointing at the typewriter, she moved her hands backwards and forwards across each other, palms downward, indicating clearly what she was suggesting.

Caryn glanced at her watch. 'It's only four o'clock,' she said
with a sigh, pouring her tea. 'I'd hate Mr Ross to come back
and find I'd taken a couple of hours off without permission.'

Marcia frowned, and then indicated the sunshine outside.
It had been another lovely day, and Caryn had the windows
wide to let in the scents and sounds of the estuary.

'I know,' she agreed now, realising it was not so difficult
to communicate as she had thought. 'Maybe later.'

Marcia hesitated and then gave a resigned nod of her head.
A raised hand indicated farewell, and she was gone, leaving
Caryn feeling infinitely less isolated.

She worked until five-thirty, and then made her way up to
the nursery. Miss Trewen had had Tristan out for a walk,
and was presently engaged in preparing his tea. Walking
across the rug where the nurse had laid him, Caryn knelt
beside her nephew, allowing herself to enjoy his wriggling
antics. In this hot weather he wore little but cotton pants and
tops, and his plump arms were honey-gold and glinting with
fine hairs. His skin was much fairer than Tristan's, she
thought, and then shrugged away the teasing reflection. His
hair, at least, resembled his father's, and on impulse she
touched its silky softness. A lurking smile lifted his mouth
and a pink tongue appeared, and Caryn felt an almost
irresistible desire to pick him up and cuddle him. She had
never felt this way about him before, and the realisation was
nonetheless disturbing for that.

She rose to her feet and at once he began to whimper. Miss
Trewen turned and then shook her finger at Caryn reprovingly.

'You've spoiled him now,' she said. 'Can you entertain
him until the kettle boils?'

Caryn hesitated, and then bent and lifted the child into her arms. Immediately his whimpering ceased, and he contented himself by poking his fingers into her mouth and tugging at the curling length of her hair. Seeing Caryn wince, Miss Trewen exclaimed:

'I hope you'll forgive me for asking, Miss Stevens, but is your hair naturally curly? I mean, it's so—attractive. I hardly like to suggest . . .'

'Unfortunately, yes,' Caryn replied without hesitation. 'It's always been like this. You can't imagine how I've longed for straight hair!'

'I can't imagine why,' retorted Miss Trewen, fingering her own mousey-grey locks. 'When I was a girl, curls were the thing, and I remember I spent pounds on perms! But all to no avail.'

Caryn smiled into Tristan's eyes. 'Is anyone ever satisfied with themselves?' she asked, stroking a long finger down his tiny nose, and started violently when a male voice answered: 'I'd be satisfied with you!'

Both women swung round, Miss Trewen rather disapprovingly, and Caryn's eyes widened when she saw Dave O'Hara standing in the half-open doorway.

'Am I intruding?' he asked innocently, and she sighed.

'What are you doing here? Angela's in Barbados.'

'Did I say I was looking for Angela?' he protested, and Miss Trewen's lips tightened as she turned back to the boiling kettle.

'I'll have Tristan's bottle ready in a moment,' she said, and Caryn hastily asked:

'Who are you looking for then?'

'I came to see Tris, but Marcia explained that he's not here,' murmured Dave, coming further into the room and attracting the baby's attention. 'So this is Tristan junior, is it? Well, well!'

Caryn could not have felt more embarrassed. 'My nephew,' she declared shortly, and was much relieved when Miss Trewen came to take him from her. 'Shall we go downstairs?'

Dave shrugged, his brow furrowing for a moment as he looked at the child, but then he followed her out of the room.

On the first landing, Caryn faced him. 'I'll tell Tris—Mr Ross you called.'

'Do that,' he agreed softly. Then: 'Come out with me!'

'Out?' She moved uncomfortably. 'What do you mean?'

'For a meal. Dinner if you like.'

Caryn shook her head. Much as she liked Dave, that moment upstairs had made her realise the difficulties she might have if she became involved with anyone.

'I'm sorry . . .'

He frowned, running a hand round inside the neck of his denim shirt. 'Do you realise if I'd asked any other girl . . .'

Caryn saw the humour of the situation. 'Did I prick your ego?'

'No.' He was indignant. 'Hey—Caryn, isn't it? I asked Angel,' he added swiftly, when she looked surprised. 'Let's go for a walk then. Where's the harm in that? I want to talk to you.'

Caryn hesitated. 'I—I——'

'You can't think of an excuse! That's good. Come on! Where's the problem?'

'What do you want to talk about?' she asked suspiciously.

'You! Me! Us! Does it matter? I'll discuss the weather, if you'll come.'

'All right,' she agreed reluctantly. 'But I'd better let Marcia know where I'm going.'

Dave accompanied her down to the lower hall and

through the door which led to the loggia. The kitchen opened off this hallway, and they found Marcia whipping up a jelly for a trifle.

'Hmm, something smells good,' Dave inserted, and Marcia cast him a reproving look. By means of mime, she managed to convey that the trifle was not for him, and he grinned goodnaturedly. 'Okay, okay,' he agreed without rancour. 'But if Tris invites me to dinner, how can I refuse?'

Caryn broke into their teasing display. 'We—I—Mr O'Hara has asked me to go for a walk with him,' she said, colouring in spite of herself, and Marcia nodded, tapping the watch on her wrist significantly, reminding her not to forget the time.

They left the house through the loggia where steep wooden steps led down to the terraced garden. Considering the gradient, Pepper had done a wonderful job of landscaping the hillside, and as well as flowers and shrubs, there were low walls and trellises, overhung with trailing vines and rambling roses.

'Shall we sit here a while?' Caryn suggested, but Dave shook his head.

'What's the matter? Can't an old lady like you stand going down to the river?' he teased, and she pulled a face at him before leading the way to the steps.

The doors of the boathouse were open, and Caryn walked along the wooden landing and peered inside. She could see the name of the yacht now. It was called *Betsy* and Caryn frowned, wondering why he had chosen that name.

'Have you heard of Betsy Ross?' asked Dave, answering her unspoken question, and she shook her head. 'She was reputed to be the woman who made the first flag depicting the Stars and Stripes,' he continued. 'And as Tris's mother is American, I guess he thought it was suitable.'

'I didn't know that.' Caryn was intrigued, and forgot for a moment her determination not to get involved in personal issues.

'Well, the story goes that before the Declaration of Independence——'

'No,' Caryn flushed, 'I don't mean that. I meant—I didn't know that—that Mr Ross's mother was an American,' she finished lamely.

'*Is*,' Dave corrected her dryly. 'She was alive and well and living in New York last time I heard of her.'

'Oh.' Caryn gave a small smile, and then emerged from the boathouse to accompany Dave along the towpath towards the estuary.

'His father was English,' he added wryly, glancing sideways at her. 'If you're interested.'

Caryn decided she had said enough about Tristan Ross and concentrated on protecting her eyes from the golden glare of the slowly sinking sun. The tide was just turning, and when they reached the confluence where the waters of the stream emptied themselves into the river, Dave suggested they took off their shoes and paddled.

Caryn looked doubtful for a moment, and then, with a shrug, she bent and turned up the cuffs of her cotton pants. Carrying her sandals, she followed Dave down the bank on to the sandy riverbed, her toes curling as the icy waters stole between them.

'Isn't this great?' he demanded, his own jeans turned up to his knees, a boyish grin making him look younger than his years.

'Great!' she conceded laughingly. 'Oooh, but it's cold!'

'You're soft,' he declared, splashing her deliberately. 'Have you ever swum in a river?'

Caryn shook her head, and he went on: 'We were playing a gig in Zurich one time, and we went swimming in the lake. Boy, was that cold! I was like an ice chip when I came out.'

Caryn grimaced. 'I've no doubt you soon found someone to warm you up again,' she mocked, and he didn't argue.

'There are always girls,' he allowed goodnaturedly.

'All willing to make themselves available,' she teased, but his regard was suddenly unnerving.

'There's making and making,' he said, and she turned abruptly away, almost overbalancing in her haste to reach the bank. He caught her as she stretched out a hand to grasp a tussock of grass to haul herself up, and his hand on her arm was compelling. 'What's with you?' he asked, frowning. 'What did I say?'

'N-nothing.' Caryn tried to be offhand. 'I'm cold, that's all.'

'You don't feel cold.'

'Well, I am.'

He let her go, but his eyes continued to hold hers. 'I like you, Caryn,' he said softly. 'I like you very much.' He paused. 'Do you think I care whose that kid is up in the nursery?'

Caryn stared at him aghast for a moment, and then the whole realisation of what he was implying came through to her. Clenching her lips, she struck him full in the face before springing up the bank and running off along the towpath. She heard him call her name, but she paid no heed, wincing as her bare feet encountered stones on the path. She didn't stop to put on her sandals, and she was panting when she reached the top of the stairs. She leant there weakly against the rail, trying to get her breath back, and as she looked up she saw Tristan Ross watching her from the open door of the loggia. His cool businesslike appearance was in strict contrast to her own dishevelment, and with trembling fingers she rolled down the cuffs of her pants and put on her sandals before walking reluctantly up the steps and into the house.

She would have preferred to have passed him without speaking, but common decency made her mutter an unconvincing: 'Good afternoon.'

'Do you usually take the steps at a gallop?' he enquired with sardonic interest, and she knew she had to make some explanation.

'I—it was late. I was in a hurry,' she replied, but his eyes had gone past her, and glancing round she saw Dave had just reached the terrace.

'Funny,' he mused dryly. 'O'Hara must have felt the same.'

Caryn gave him a resentful look. 'All right, we were together.'

'And he made a pass at you?'

She hesitated. 'If you like.'

Tristan stepped in front of her. 'Did he or didn't he?'

Caryn looked up at him mutinously. 'If you must know, he implied that—that the baby was mine.'

He inclined his head, his mouth moving mockingly. 'And I would hazard from the marks I can see on his cheek that you slapped his face,' he drawled in a low tone so that Dave, coming up the steps into the loggia, should not overhear him. 'When are you going to learn that lashing out at people solves nothing?'

'I suppose you have a better solution!' she declared, and then, hearing Dave's footsteps, went past Tristan and into the main body of the house. But she had the uneasy suspicion that she was giving in to cowardice and little else. And it was doubly galling when she heard how the two men greeted one another. Obviously, whatever she thought, Tristan bore Dave no ill will.

CHAPTER SIX

The following week Caryn met Tristan's editor, Mike Ramsey, and his cameraman, Phil Thornton. Because of his experience in television, on both sides of the camera, Tristan produced and directed his own films, but Mike was both his editor and his friend. A lot of the groundwork for the series of programmes had been accomplished now, but the format for presenting the information had still to be worked out. The introductory programme which dealt mainly with the economic climate of the rest of the Common Market countries was already 'in the can' as they termed it, but it was the other five which were going to present the most difficulties, subject as they were to the ever-changing economic patterns in the country.

Because they chose to work at Druid's Fleet, Caryn was made very conscious of her presence in Tristan's study, and although he protested she was not in the way, she insisted on moving her typewriter out to the loggia and working there. Their discussions were becoming a distraction to her anyway, and she did not want to feel any reluctant admiration for her employer's grasp of the situation or find herself agreeing with any of his ideas. She had no idea how long he intended to employ her, but she was prepared to stay indefinitely, if necessary, if it meant assuring the child of its rightful home, and the only way their association could continue was if the detachment between them could be maintained. After all, how could she expect an outsider to accept the situation if she couldn't accept it herself? All the same, there were occasions when she wondered exactly what she was doing here, and an awful feeling of depression swept over her. But fortunately those occasions were few and far between. Yet her position was nebulous, and she knew Miss Trewen, if not Marcia, considered her relationship with Tristan questionable.

About three weeks after her installation at Druid's Fleet, Tristan came into the loggia one morning while she was drinking her coffee. It was a misty morning, with the drifting dampness of rain spoiling the view from the windows and giving everything a cool, clammy feel.

Since he had been working at home, she had got used to seeing him in jeans and casual knitted shirts, but this morning he was wearing a brown vicuna lounge suit, whose closely-woven threads moulded the width of his shoulders and the narrow muscles of his thighs, and a curious pang, which she quickly suppressed, assailed her at the realisation he must beleaving again.

'How are you getting on?' he enquired, standing before her, the epitome of the successful male, and she lifted her eyes from their involuntary contemplation of his lean body.

'I've nearly finished this estimate——'

'No. I'm sorry . . .' It was unlike him to be so formal, and she waited half anxiously for him to explain what he meant: 'I was wondering whether you were enjoying the work, or whether you found it—repetitive.'

'Repetitive?' Caryn shook her head. 'No.' She paused: 'Why?'

He frowned. 'You've been typing re-drafts until you must practically know them off by heart.'

'I don't mind,' she said, somewhat stiffly, wondering what was coming next.

'Perhaps not.' He considered her thoughtfully. 'But it did occur to me that when we had that little—argument over

Miss Trewen, I omitted to mention what free time and salary you should have.'

Caryn was amazed at the weak relief that filled her. 'I—I have free time. When you're away——'

'—you go on working,' he finished dryly. 'Sometimes into the evenings. Marcia doesn't miss much.'

'I haven't complained.'

'Did I say you had?' He gave her a look of resignation. 'I'm not here to criticise you, Miss Stevens, merely to assure myself that I'm not working you too hard.'

Caryn had no answer to this, and half impatiently he moved away from her to stand staring out at the misty morning. His hair had grown in the weeks since she had been here, and now overlapped his collar at the back, its straight smoothness in direct contrast to her own unruly curls. She found herself wondering how she would have felt if he had chosen to pay attention to her. Without Loren's previous experience to guide her, she realised with honesty she might well have become attracted to the man, but would she, like her sister, have given in to him? Would she have risked becoming pregnant on the offchance that he might be prepared to do the decent thing and marry her? Of course, Loren could have had an abortion. She had no doubt that given the information a doctor might well have been prepared to terminate the life that was threatening to destroy hers. But curiously, or perhaps not so curiously, Loren hadn't wanted that, and then it was too late ... Even so, neither of them had imagined that anything could go wrong at the birth in these enlightened times, and the undetected virus which had swept through the hospital was one of those chances in a million ...

Tristan turned and found her gazing in his direction. With scarcely concealed embarrassment, she quickly swit-

ched her attention to the pile of letters still awaiting her
attention, shuffling them almost nervously. What was he
waiting for? Had he something else to say?

'We're leaving for London in a few minutes,' he said at
last, and she permitted herself to look at him again.

'Yes?'

'Yes.' He came towards the desk again. 'I'll be filming
there until Friday. As I've paid two months' salary into an
account for you at the bank in Port Edward, I suggest you
take a couple of days off while I'm away.' He paused. 'Take
your nephew out. Have a picnic. I'm sure Miss Trewen
would love it.'

'I'm not here to take—take the baby for picnics, Mr Ross,'
she demurred firmly, and his lips tightened.

'Call him Tristan, for God's sake!' he snapped. 'That is
his name. Or is it so distasteful to you?'

'All right. I'm not here to take *Tristan* for picnics.'

He sighed in exasperation. 'No. You're my employee. And
I'll decide what you do.'

'I'm your secretary, Mr Ross, nothing else.'

'No?' He came to rest his hands on the table she was
working on, pushing his face so close to hers that she had to
force herself not to move her chair back to get away from
him. 'You're forgetting the conditions.'

Caryn could see every pore in his face—the deep-set eyes,
with their tawny streaks, narrow cheekbones, his thin upper
lip and fuller, sensual lower one. His mouth fascinated her
and his breath was warm against her temple. Her pulse fluttered nervously, and the eyes she raised to his held little of
the angry determination she was trying to hold on to.

He stared at her grimly for several seconds, and then with
an oath he straightened. 'Damn you, Caryn, why should I
care if you work yourself to death?'

It was the first time he had used her Christian name, and it came strangely from his lips. It revealed that he did not think of her as 'Miss Stevens' at all, and the knowledge was disturbing.

Needing to do something, she pushed back her chair and got to her feet. 'I'm sorry if you think I'm ungrateful——' she began, only to have him harshly break in on her.

'Oh, I think that!' he declared. 'I also think it's time I stopped pussyfooting around and told you flatly that your sister was not the plaster saint you appear to think her. Angel told me I should tell you, but I was reluctant to do so. But now . . . What the hell!'

'I don't want to hear your biased opinions,' she exclaimed tremulously, but he ignored her.

'From the minute Loren came here, she began to cause problems, of one kind or another,' he incised. 'She was lazy and careless, and as for loving me . . .' He shook his head. 'She loved this way of life. She liked this house, and the people who came into it. She may even have regarded me as a meal-ticket, but that's all.'

'You were attracted to her . . .'

'She was eighteen, Caryn! Younger than my own daughter! I might have been fooled into feeling sympathy for her, but I was not sexually attracted to her!'

Caryn bent her head. 'Why are you telling me this? We've already aired our opinions, and we'll never agree.'

'Because I felt we knew each other better now,' he snapped coldly. 'Obviously I was wrong.'

'All you've told me is that Loren wasn't any good at her job. You should have fired her.'

'I did!' he declared angrily.

'When you thought she might be pregnant!'

'Oh, Lord!' He strode across the room towards the door.

'Forget it. Forget everything I said. I'll see you on Friday.'

Surprisingly, after he had gone all Caryn could remember was the look of anguish on his face as he left her. But what had he expected after all? Just because he had proved to be a considerate and intelligent employer did not change his moral image. He was used to wearing a mask before the cameras. How easy it must be for him to adopt the kind of pose he knew she would most want to see.

The weather changed again the following day, and on impulse Caryn decided to suggest a picnic to Miss Trewen. The nurse was most enthusiastic, and Marcia was prevailed upon to provide them with a hamper to take to the beach. Caryn asked the housekeeper to join them, but she demurred, and Caryn guessed that Marcia was shy of meeting other people.

They took the car and drove to Heron's Cove, a beauty spot near Caldy Sands, some ten miles distant. There were a number of cars already parked on the headland, and with each of them carrying a handle of the carrycot where Tristan lay gurgling, Caryn and Miss Trewen descended the stone steps to the cove.

Caryn was wearing her swimsuit, and after Miss Trewen and her charge were settled on the rug they had brought, she stripped off her denim skirt and cotton vest to reveal a dark blue bikini.

'Oh, my!' Miss Trewen looked up at her in surprise. 'Aren't you slim!'

'After having a baby, do you mean?' Caryn asked slyly, and Miss Trewen looked embarrassed.

'I—why—I never meant——'

'It's all right, Miss Trewen.' Caryn took pity on her. 'But Tristan's really not my child, you know. He was my sister Loren's son. She died only a few days after he was born.'

Miss Trewen shook her head. 'A tragedy!' she murmured. Then: 'But Mr Ross has been—very kind to you. Almost like—one of the family.'

Caryn decided the conversation had gone far enough. 'He has been a good friend,' she conceded lightly, and curtailed the discussion by running down the beach and into the chilly waters of Carmarthen Bay.

The next day was equally hot, and from her desk in Tristan's study, Caryn envied the holidaymakers she could see sunbathing on the decks of their sailing dinghies or swimming in the cool waters of the estuary. Even the village had a continental charm in the bright sunlight, and coloured blinds had appeared that gave it a curiously alien appearance.

Even wearing the minimum amount of clothing Caryn was sweating, and after lunching with Miss Trewen in the nursery, she suggested they went down to the beach again.

'Oh, not me. Not today,' declared the nurse, fanning herself. 'It's much too hot for the beach, and we had enough sun yesterday.'

Caryn glanced towards Tristan's cot and sighed. Miss Trewen was probably right. It was too hot for the beach, but she longed to submerge her body in cool water, and swimming in the estuary seemed too close to home somehow.

Telling Marcia she would be back by five, she put on her swimsuit, collected a towel and drove away. Taking the road she had traversed the day before, she drove past Heron's Cove and keeping the sea in view, turned on to a narrow peninsula that projected itself into the blue-green waters. There were no tarmac car-parks here, and she reached a spot which looked interesting and just left the Renault parked on the grassy cliffs.

As she scrambled down to the cove hidden beneath the curve of the rocky headland, she reflected that it was just as

well Miss Trewen was not with her. The nurse could never
have negotiated such a precarious path, even without the
daunting presence of the carrycot. Still, she thought soberly,
if Miss Trewen had been with her, she would in all probability have returned to Heron's Cove.

At the foot of the cliffs, seaweed-strewn rocks stretched
out into foam-flecked water. Definitely not a swimming area,
she decided ruefully, but she could wade into the waves and
cool herself that way.

Her skirt and top came off, and she paddled at the water's
edge. It was quite a novelty being entirely alone, although
she did not dismiss the awareness of taking no unnecessary
risks for that very reason.

After she had soaked herself thoroughly, and her hair was
clinging wetly about her shoulders, she returned to the
pebbly beach and finding a spot less lumpy than some others,
she stretched her legs on the towel and reached for her skin
lotion.

Apart from the occasional cries of the gulls that nested in
the upper reaches of the cliffs, the only sounds were those of
the sea on the rocks, and an occasional insect that was
attracted by the scent of the seaweed. She half wished she
had brought her transistor, and then inwardly chided herself
for needing more than the natural sounds around her. She
tried to imagine what it must be like to be marooned on a
desert island, and decided it was not a prospect she would
welcome.

Time passed, and the spot where she was lying became
shadowed by the headland, providing a welcome respite
from the direct glare of the sun. Caryn put a hand behind
her head, and stared at the distant horizon, the blue of the
ocean lost in a haze that melted into sky without any evident
distinction. Tristan was a little like that, she reflected frown-

ingly, shifting from one mood to another for no adequate reason.

But she didn't want to think about him, she decided impatiently. She didn't want to think that she was doing as he had suggested and taking time off while he was away, and she didn't want to find herself wondering what he was doing right now.

Even so, she couldn't help speculating upon who might be the woman in his life at the moment. Since she came to Druid's Fleet, he had entertained no one, to her knowledge, but his two television colleagues and Dave O'Hara.

She sighed. Of course, he hadn't been at the house all the time, and even when he was there, he often went out in the evenings. No doubt there was some woman in the background, someone he would consider suitable to become the second Mrs Ross, but as yet she had not heard of her. Since coming to Wales she had read few newspapers, however, and as most of her information about him had come from the gossip columns, she was probably out of touch.

The glare of sun on sea was very bright, and reluctantly her eyes closed. She felt very warm and comfortable, and even the uncertainty of her position at Druid's Fleet seemed far away and no longer so important . . .

It was much different when she opened her eyes again. It was cold for one thing, and the sun was no longer anything more than a shifting of shadows on the ocean. Impatiently she reached for her watch. She had taken it off when she went wading, putting it into the pocket of her skirt, and she stared disbelievingly at the square masculine face. It was after six. She had slept for two hours!

Scrambling to her feet, she tugged the striped cotton vest over her head and pulled on the denim skirt. Her bathing suit had dried on her, and gathering up her towel and bag, she turned to the cliff path.

It was more rugged going up than coming down, but when she looked back at the cove she thought how fortunate it was that the tide had not come right in and trapped her by the rocks. She had been rather foolhardy falling asleep, and she hoped Marcia had not worried about her. The roads were busy as she drove back to Port Edward. Dozens of holidaymakers had taken advantage of the good weather to go down to the beaches, and by the time she arrived back at Druid's Fleet it was almost half past seven. Her stomach was protesting at the long period without food, and she was looking forward to her supper with real enthusiasm.

A grey Mercedes was parked to one side of the door, and her senses sharpened. She knew it was Tristan's car, although it was unusual for him to leave it parked out in the front. A steep slope led down to a huge garage, and invariably he rolled the big car into that barn-like shelter.

'Damn!' she swore silently to herself, as she stopped the Renault and switched off the engine. He hadn't been expected back until tomorrow. Now he would know that she had been enjoying herself in his absence.

She thrust open her door and got out, collecting her belongings from the back seat and slamming the door behind her. The sound must have attracted attention because almost immediately the porch door opened and Marcia's anxious face appeared. She looked so relieved to see Caryn that the girl felt contrite, and she hastened towards her apologetically.

'I know, I know,' she said. 'I'm late. I'm sorry.'

Marcia shook her head expressively, and then gestured for Caryn to come inside, and as she did so Tristan came up the stairs from the lower landing. For once he looked less than controlled, his beige silk shirt unbuttoned down his chest, his navy trousers stained with mud and grass stains.

'*Caryn!*' he said incredulously, then more aggressively: 'Where the hell have you been?'

Caryn glanced round at Marcia closing the door behind her. 'I'm sorry,' she exclaimed. 'I fell asleep——'

'You did *what*!' Tristan had reached her now, and she could smell the sweating heat of his body which was also not normal for him.

'I—fell asleep. On the beach——'

'What beach?'

'What beach?' She looked up at him confusedly. 'I don't know what beach.'

'Then you bloody well ought to,' he swore violently, and she took an automatic step backward.

'I don't know what you're getting so annoyed about,' she protested. 'I'm late, I know, but——'

'Late?' He made an exasperated sound. 'You told Marcia you'd be back by five.'

'I know I did.' Caryn was beginning to feel annoyed herself. 'So what? I didn't know you were coming back today. If you have some work for me——'

'To hell with work!' he snapped savagely, and then turned away, raking a slightly unsteady hand through his hair. He seemed to be trying to calm himself, and when he turned back to her he had himself in control. 'All right,' he said heavily. 'All right. Perhaps I'm over-reacting.' He paused. 'I expect you're hungry.' His gaze flicked to Marcia. 'Prepare a tray for two, would you? And fetch it to the sitting room.'

Caryn realised her own palms were sweating, and they slipped unpleasantly along the strap of her bag. 'If you don't mind, I'll take a shower,' she said, aware that her voice sounded stiff. 'Then perhaps I could have my supper in my room . . .'

'You'll have your supper in the sitting room with me,' retorted Tristan harshly, and without waiting for her protest, he climbed the stairs to the upper landing, disappearing into the north wing.

After he had gone, Marcia spread her hands helplessly, and, nodding, Caryn followed him up the stairs. But much more slowly.

Miss Trewen came to her room as Caryn was sitting before her dressing table applying a moisturiser to her face. The salt air had dried her skin in spite of the lotion she had spread so liberally, and it was good to feel the tautness relaxing under the lanolin. She was only wearing a thin cotton robe when the knock came at the door, and she called: 'Who is it?' in slightly uneasy tones.

'Only me,' ventured the nurse, tentatively opening the door, and Caryn beckoned her inside. 'I heard the commotion downstairs. Where have you been?'

Caryn sighed. 'I went to the beach. Not Heron's Cove,' she added quickly, 'just an inlet I found off the beaten track.'

'I see.' Miss Trewen threaded her fingers together. 'That would explain it, of course.'

'Explain what?'

Caryn frowned, and the older woman shook her head reprovingly. 'Why Mr Ross didn't find you,' she declared.

'He's been looking!' exclaimed Caryn disbelievingly, and when Miss Trewen nodded, went on: 'But why?'

'I believe you had told Marcia——'

'—that I'd be back by five,' Caryn finished impatiently. 'Yes, I know that. But honestly, I'm not a child——'

'Nevertheless, Mr Ross said there were some dangerous

coves around here, and he was afraid you might get trapped by the incoming tide.'

'I see.' Caryn turned back to study her reflection without pleasure. It didn't fit her image of Tristan Ross to think of him as a man who cared about his employees' welfare, but remembering his grass-stained trousers she wondered uneasily if he had climbed down some cliff face looking for her.

'He was very worried,' continued Miss Trewen, adding to the feelings of guilt Caryn was already experiencing. 'And when we heard that news report . . .'

'What news report?' Caryn turned to stare at her.

'About those two boys.' Miss Trewen frowned. 'I thought that's what Mr Ross was telling you downstairs.'

'What two boys?' exclaimed Caryn, trying to be patient, and Miss Trewen made a gesture of regret.

'Two boys were drowned late this afternoon in Carmarthen Bay. I believe their dinghy had overturned and they'd tried to swim for the shore, but . . .' she shook her head, 'they didn't make it.'

'Oh, lord!' Caryn swung round to rest her elbows on the dressing table, cupping her chin in her hands. 'If only I'd known . . .'

Miss Trewen nodded. 'Still, I don't suppose you could have helped them,' she reassured her absently, and Caryn had to hide the unwilling smile that tugged at her lips. It was so easy for Miss Trewen. She didn't get involved in personal relationships, while she . . .

Caryn determinedly smoothed the cream into her temples, and after assuring herself that the girl had suffered no ill effects from her outing, Miss Trewen left her, saying there was a television programme she wanted to see.

After brushing her hair into some semblance of order,

Caryn opened the wardrobe and extracted a cream Dacron button-through dress that was loose and sleeveless, and displayed her gipsy darkness to advantage. Then, after sliding her bare feet into leather-thonged sandals, she went downstairs.

Tristan was already in the sitting room, helping himself to a Scotch from a tray of bottles and glasses on a table in the corner. He had changed, too, and his close-fitting velvet pants couldn't help but draw attention to the lean length of his legs. For once he wasn't wearing a jacket, and his black silk shirt threw his ash-fair hair into prominence. He, too, had had a shower, and droplets of water still glinted on the artificially darkened strands.

He looked round when she entered the room, and at once she was nervous. This was the first time their being together had been anything less than businesslike, and he must know the effect he had on women. It wasn't anything he did precisely, or even anything he said. He just had a certain *presence* that made her immediately aware of her own femininity. It made her stiffen towards him, and his casual offer of a drink was accepted through taut lips.

'Sherry, please,' she said, and although he raised his eyebrows, he made no demur. 'Dry, if you have it.'

He poured a schooner of the pale golden liquid and carried it across to her, his own half empty tumbler held casually in his other hand.

He wasn't wearing a tie this evening, and in the opened neck of his shirt she could see a narrow leather necklet. Something was suspended from it, but she couldn't see what, and realising she was staring, she quickly applied her attention to the sherry.

He studied her discomposure with narrowed eyes for a moment, and then he turned to the windows to stare out broodingly over the estuary. When he looked round again she had moved away from him and was hovering near the empty fireplace.

'Exactly where did you go this afternoon?' he enquired, before swallowing the remainder of the Scotch in his glass at a gulp, and she moved her shoulders uncomfortably.

'I'm not sure. I drove on to a peninsula. I just stopped the car and climbed down to some cove.' She paused, and then added swiftly: 'I'm sorry if I—alarmed you. I—didn't know about the two boys who were drowned.'

He frowned. 'You do now.'

'Miss Trewen told me. She said you'd gone looking for me.'

He walked slowly back to the table and poured himself another Scotch. With his back to her, he said dryly: 'And I suppose you didn't believe her.'

'No!' Caryn made a sound of protest. 'I mean—of course I believed her.'

'Did you?' He turned and surveyed her sardonically. 'And what did you think, I wonder? That I was just protecting my investment? That I wouldn't want to lose such a good secretary?'

Caryn didn't answer this, and somewhat restlessly, he paced back to the windows again. Watching him, she sensed his impatience, and wondered uneasily whether he was regretting employing her.

'I finished the drafts of the two scripts you left me, and the letters that came while you were away——' she offered, and he scowled.

'Tell me tomorrow,' he interrupted her abruptly, and she raised her glass to her lips with an unpleasant feeling of reproof.

It was with some relief she welcomed Marcia's appearance

with the tray. She set it down on the low table near one of
the velvet couches, and the succulent aroma of chicken cas-
serole came to Caryn's nostrils. The housekeeper assured
herself that they could help themselves and then mimed that
she would bring the coffee later.

Caryn hesitated a moment after Marcia had gone, and
then said awkwardly: 'Shall I?'

Tristan shrugged. 'Please do!' and with some misgivings
she seated herself on the couch beside the tray.

There was some fresh salmon to start with, but Tristan
didn't want any and she found her own appetite was de-
pleted by his indifference. She turned instead to the cas-
serole, and spooned flaky rice on to a plate before covering it
with some of the milk-white chicken nestling in its creamy
sauce. A sprig of parsley added colour to the dish, and to her
consternation, when she held the plate out to Tristan, he
came and seated himself on the couch beside her. But before
eating, he picked up the bottle of wine that also occupied a
corner of the tray and expertly removed the cork.

'Do you like Riesling?' he asked, as he poured some of the
colourless liquid into a tall glass, and she managed a faint
murmur of acquiescence.

His weight on the couch beside her was infinitely more
disturbing than any amount of wine could have been, she reflected, forking a sliver of chicken into her mouth. She was
supremely conscious of his thigh only inches from her own
on the soft velvet cushion, and the fleeting penetration of the
amber eyes which were occasionally cast in her direction.

'Is it good?' he asked once when she allowed her tongue to
curl out and rescue a grain of rice from her upper lip, and
she coloured in embarrassment.

'Very good,' she replied quickly, but his expression as he
applied himself to his own meal was wry.

Caryn felt infinitely better with some food inside her. The fluttery sensation in the region of her solar plexus was no longer so evident, and she decided her nerves were primarily caused by hunger.

A delectable raspberry pudding awaited for dessert, but Tristan declined to try any of this and Caryn contented herself by taking a small helping for herself. Tristan refilled her wine glass even though only a small amount had been drunk out of it, and proceeded to finish the bottle. He lay back against the apricot upholstery, holding his glass up to the light and studying her through it.

Caryn soon ate the pudding, and wiped her mouth feeling replete. In spite of everything, she had enjoyed it, and when Marcia came to clear and fetch the coffee, she offered her compliments. The housekeeper allowed a small smile to lift her lips, and went away again, leaving Caryn to handle the coffee cups.

'How do you like it?' she asked, looking at Tristan, the coffee pot in her hand.

'How do I like what?' he countered lazily, and something in his expression made her look away from him. At once, he straightened away from the cushions and said: 'Black. With sugar!' as though regretting his momentary baiting.

Caryn filled his cup and spooned brown sugar into it. 'Is that all right?'

'Perfect,' he assured her, somewhat sardonically. Then: 'Tell me how long you worked for Laurence Mellor.'

His question was so unexpected that she stared at him. 'Don't you know? I thought you had a dossier on all your employees.'

He returned her stare steadily. 'I'm asking you.'

Immediately Caryn felt uneasy. 'Four years,' she replied shortly. 'Why do you want to know?'

He didn't answer this, but said instead: 'He wanted to marry you, didn't he?'

'How do you know that?'

Her involuntary exclamation was an admission, and he knew it. 'How about—he told me?'

'I don't believe that.'

His mouth twisted with wry humour. 'No. You wouldn't.'

Caryn put down her coffee cup and looked at him uncomfortably. 'Are you going to tell me?'

He set his glass down and sat with his legs apart, his arms resting along his thighs. 'I guessed,' he told her evenly. 'Do you believe that?'

Caryn's brow furrowed. 'I don't know . . .'

He shrugged. 'Your previous employer was not exactly unstinting in his praise of you. There had to be one of two reasons. A—you were no good at the job; or B—he was personally involved with you. Obviously, it wasn't the former, so it had to be the latter.'

Caryn's lips tightened. 'You're very clever!' But it wasn't a commendation.

He sighed. 'No, I'm not. Just practical.'

'Calculating!'

'If you like. It pays to calculate the odds in my job.'

Caryn examined her hands lying in her lap. 'Was that why you dismissed Loren?' she asked, and heard his angry intake of breath.

'Will you never leave that alone?' he exclaimed harshly. 'I've told you about Loren. For God's sake, I'm supporting her child, aren't I? What more do you want of me?'

Caryn quivered. 'An—an admission . . .'

'What of? Guilt? Remorse?' He turned towards her angrily. 'What do I have to feel guilty about? What remorse should I feel?'

'Only you know that,' she retorted shakily.

'You have such an opinion of me, haven't you?' he pursued. 'What do I have to do to prove to you that I'm not the monster you think I am?'

Cary's mouth was dry, and her breath rasped painfully in her throat. 'You don't have to prove anything to me,' she got out raggedly, but clearly he didn't believe her.

'Do you know what I'm tempted to do?' he demanded, and suddenly his eyes were moving over her, lingering insinuatingly on the buttoned neckline of her dress, moving down over her swiftly rising breasts to where her hands plucked nervously at her skirt. He had never looked at her like this before, and she was made heatedly aware of the power he could exert when he chose to do so.

'I think it's time I went up to my room,' she declared, half rising to her feet, but his hand on her knee compelled her to remain where she was.

'Coward,' he said softly, mockery tinging his words. 'What do you think I'm going to do to you? What are you afraid of? You can always slap my face.'

'Mr Ross——'

'Yes, Miss Stevens?'

'Will you let go of my knee?'

'No.' He moved along the couch towards her, and her breathing almost stopped it, was so shallow. 'Why should I? You think the worst of me. Why shouldn't I prove it?'

'This is ridiculous! If you don't let me go——'

'Yes? What will you do? Call for help? Who will help you? Marcia? I don't think so. Miss Trewen? Hardly. Tristan? Unfortunately not.'

When she would have pushed him away, his hand imprisoned both of hers, and she was helpless before him, like a mouse caught in a trap.

'Mmm, this is nice,' he murmured, inhaling her perfume. 'Now what shall we do?'

Caryn clenched her teeth. 'Let me go!'

'And what will you do?' He waited for her reply. 'Scratch my eyes out?'

'It's nothing more than you deserve!' she panted, and as suddenly as he had taken hold of her she was free again.

But now weakness had taken hold of her lower limbs, and it seemed incredibly difficult to summon the energy to rise from the couch. Instead, he continued to look at her, the humour disappearing from his mouth as she returned his stare.

Needing something to hold on to, Caryn broke into words: 'Is—is your daughter enjoying her holiday?' she stammered foolishly, and he closed his eyes against the timidity of her expression.

'Oh, Caryn!' he groaned, opening his eyes again. He ran a hand round the back of his neck, tipping his head back flexingly, and then got up from the couch. 'Yes, she's enjoying her holiday,' he said flatly. 'Do you want another drink?'

'What? Oh, no.' Caryn shook her head, and with a shrug he went to pour himself another Scotch.

When he turned, she had risen to her feet, the burgeoning peaks of her breasts clearly outlined against the fine material of her dress.

'You're leaving,' he remarked, without expression. 'Yes. Run away, little girl!'

Caryn caught her breath. 'I don't like your insinuation, Mr Ross. If this is how you make your conquests, I'm sorry I've been wasting your time!'

His eyes narrowed, the thick lashes hiding the tawny irises. 'Is that what you think, Miss Stevens?' he drawled. 'Should I disillusion you?'

'You disillusioned me a long time ago,' she retorted, and reluctant admiration touched his lips.

'*Touché!*' He put down his glass. 'But I don't think you know the meaning of the word.'

'I know——' she was declaring vehemently, when she realised he had moved so that he was between her and the door.

'What do you know, I wonder?' he taunted. 'I don't believe you've ever slept with a man.'

Caryn's face burned. 'And—and is that your criterion?' she demanded unsteadily. 'I'll have you know——' She broke off briefly as he came towards her, his hands closing round her upper arms, firm and unyielding, but she forced herself to go on: '—there are more important things in life than going to bed with—with some arrogant male——'

Her words were punctuated by gulps as he bent his head towards her, his lips barely stroking the warm curve of her neck, the sun-tanned skin of her shoulder revealed by the sleeveless dress. She wanted to struggle, but it didn't seem an adult thing to do, and she continued talking in a determined effort to show him he really was wasting his time with her.

'—you can't understand that, of course. You—you show a—a fine contempt for my sex, taking—taking them without respect or—or love——'

His tongue probed the hollow of her ear, and a quiver of emotion ran through her. His alcohol-scented breath was not unpleasant, and as he drew her closer she could feel the powerful muscles of his thighs pressing against hers. His lips trailed along the curve of her jawline, but when they touched the corner of her mouth she realised that, adult or not, she had to get away from him.

She opened her mouth to speak again, and then gasped as his mouth covered hers, the dark sweetness of his kiss invading and intimate. The hardness of his chest was crushing her breasts, but it was a pleasurable sensation, and his hands were cupping the back of her head, his thumbs probing the sensitive hollows behind her ears. Her clenched fists pressed determinedly to her sides jerked resistingly, but when his kiss hardened into passion, they reached towards him, spreading over his chest to the nape of his neck. Her unconscious yielding made him almost lose his balance, and he parted his legs to support them both, drawing her even closer between.

The shrilling of the telephone was both harsh and unwelcome, and sobering. Caryn opened her eyes to find Tristan closing his, and with a groan of protest he put her from him and went to answer it. Only then did she become aware that several buttons on her dress were unfastened, and her pulses throbbed as she saw the marks of his fingers visible on her body.

His back was to her as he picked up the receiver, and she looked longingly towards the door. Apart from anything else, she didn't want to eavesdrop on his conversation, she told herself, not wanting to acknowledge the awful sense of self-disgust that was sweeping over her. After everything she knew about him, she thought with dismay. That she should have let him touch her . . .

He turned, as if sensing her withdrawal, and his eyes revealed the cynical twist of his expression. 'Yes,' he was saying, to whoever it was on the phone, 'I know. Yes. Well, it's been pretty hectic. I know that, but——'

Caryn looked away from him, and walked jerkily towards

the windows, and as if impatient to get away, she heard him making some excuse about not being able to come over because he was tied up at the moment. Who was asking? she wondered bitterly. Another woman!

She heard the receiver being replaced, and half afraid he would come across to her and try to take up where he left off, she swung round.

'I'm sorry about that,' he remarked, fingering the leather cord around his neck, and she glimpsed the copper amulet that was attached to it. 'I'm afraid I've been neglecting people lately.'

Caryn had no intention of entering into a conversation with him. 'I'm rather tired,' she said coldly. 'Is it all right if I go to bed now?'

Hunching his shoulders, he pushed his hands into the pockets of his pants. 'Of course,' he agreed, inclining his head, and feeling curiously let down, Caryn made for the door. But before she opened it, he said: 'I suppose I've damned myself beyond all redemption!' and she looked back at him half uncertainly.

Then she gathered her composure. 'You simply proved the kind of man you are.'

His expression grew mocking. 'How convenient! Would it do any good to tell you that I had no intention of making love to you?'

'It's a little late——'

'No.' He shook his head. 'You mistake my meaning. I meant I didn't mean to—go to bed with you.'

Caryn gasped indignantly. 'I do not go to bed with men!'

'You will,' he assured her laconically, and then, as if bored by the conversation, he went to rescue the drink he had poured earlier.

Caryn hesitated. Whichever way she turned, he seemed to

get the better of her. And in spite of everything that had gone before, she was suddenly loath to leave him thinking he had had the last word.

'You—you believe I'd have gone to bed with you, don't you?' she persisted woodenly, and he turned to her, swallowing some of the whisky from his glass as he did so.

He wiped his mouth on the back of his hand, and then he said quietly: 'I wouldn't presume to anticipate such a thing. Why should you think I would?'

Caryn shifted from one foot to the other. 'But you said——'

'If you choose to interpret my words that way...' he shrugged, 'I can't stop you.'

'Why—why, you——'

He smiled rather sardonically. 'Go on, say it. It's been said before.'

'I bet it has!'

'But not by a woman,' he added mockingly, and without another word, she pulled open the door and left him.

CHAPTER SEVEN

During the following two weeks, Caryn saw nothing of her employer, and she told herself she was glad. The morning after the evening she had spent in his company, she had awakened with a definite feeling of apprehension, and it had not dispersed until she had discovered that Tristan had left for London again as abruptly as he had appeared. Exactly why he had come to Wales, she had no way of knowing, and she eventually assumed he had been assuring himself that she had plenty to do in his absence. Obviously after she had retired he had done some work, because in the morning she found several tapes awaiting her attention. At least his departure gave her a respite, and she supposed she ought to thank him for that.

Dave O'Hara turned up one afternoon towards the end of the second week and came strolling into the sitting room where Caryn was engaged in checking a report Tristan had left her to type. She wasn't enthusiastic at seeing him, but his whimsical smile begged forgiveness and she laid the report aside resignedly.

'How are you?' he asked, halting in the middle of the floor, his hands tucked carelessly into the pockets of a nylon jerkin he was wearing.

'I'm fine,' she replied, crossing her slim legs, realising as she did so that living by the sea was making her skin more gipsy-like than ever. 'What are you doing here?'

'Looking for you,' he declared honestly. 'I've got the bike outside. Come for a ride with me!'

'On a bike!' she exclaimed disbelievingly, and he laughed. 'A motor-bike! You know—put-put!'

Caryn had to smile at this, but she shook her head. 'I'm sorry, I can't.'

'Why not? You're not so busy. Tris hasn't been home for a couple of weeks.'

'How do you know that?'

'He told me.'

She stiffened. 'When?'

'At his pad. Last Sunday.'

'You were at Tri—Mr Ross's apartment last Sunday?'

'Sure,' Dave nodded, then pulled a reflective face. 'That was some party he gave.'

'He gave a party?'

Caryn felt singularly stupid repeating everything he said, but somehow she had not associated Tristan's absence with parties. And yet why shouldn't he entertain? Why *wouldn't* he? He was invited to plenty of functions, and he did know a lot of people.

She was annoyed now that she had let Dave see how his news had affected her, and his casual: 'Didn't you know?' left her in no doubt that he already knew the answer.

'It's nothing to do with me,' she demurred, picking up her typing again and shuffling the pages together. 'Now, if you'll excuse me . . .'

'Aw, come on!' Dave stepped in front of her as she rose to pass him. 'Tris will be here at the weekend and then you'll tell me you have even less time.'

Caryn's fingers stilled. 'Er—Mr Ross is—coming here? At the weekend?'

Dave nodded impatiently. 'Yeah. He's bringing Melanie down for the weekend.'

Caryn's lips formed the word: 'Melanie?'

'Melanie Forbes! Surely you've heard of her.'

'*That* Melanie!' Caryn swallowed convulsively. Of course

she had heard of Melanie Forbes. Who hadn't? She was a singer who had recently made her name as an actress as well, and because she was beautiful as well as talented her picture was always appearing in the papers. The fact that her father was Sir George Forbes had nothing to do with it, they said, even if he did run one of the larger television companies and spent a good deal of his time and money financing charity performances.

'Yes, that Melanie!' agreed Dave now, scuffing his boot against the soft carpet. 'So you're really determined not to come out with me?'

Caryn hesitated. Dave's news about Tristan bringing this girl down here for the weekend was disturbing, and she told herself it was because she was thinking of her nephew. Nevertheless, her taste for industry had waned somewhat, and she wasn't looking forward at all to the next few days.

Sensing her indecision, Dave pressed his advantage: 'You'd enjoy a ride, Caryn. It's stuffy in here. You'd be out in the open air—feeling the wind against your skin! You can always work at the weekend,' he added slyly.

Caryn looked at him uncertainly. 'I don't have a helmet.'

'Tris does. Borrow his.'

'I don't know where it is.'

'I'd guess it's in the garage,' Dave asserted dryly. 'Well? Are you coming?'

'All right.' Caryn gave in, but she looked down rather regretfully at her cotton sundress. 'I'll have to change.'

'Jeans and a shirt,' declared Dave firmly. 'That's all you need. I can supply the rest.' He grinned. 'And you can make what you like of that!'

Marcia looked disapproving when Caryn told her where she was going. For once she got her little notebook off the dresser in the kitchen and wrote: *TELL HIM NOT TO DRIVE TOO FAST!* in capital letters.

'I will,' said Caryn, touched by the woman's concern, and wondered not for the first time how Marcia, with her looks, came to be anyone's housekeeper.

Dave had recovered the helmet, and Caryn tried it on. It was a little big for her, but the strap tightened it under her chin. She felt ridiculous, and said so, but Dave just turned his thumbs up and grinned his approval.

Certainly, she decided later that afternoon, a motor-bike could weave its way through busy traffic more easily than a car. On roads jammed with holidaymakers, they passed them all, and reached the village of St Gifford in the late afternoon.

'Where are we going?' she asked, leaning over Dave's shoulder to voice the question, and he grinned.

'We're going to a party,' he averred, and saw her look of dismay before he added swiftly: 'Calm down! I'll have you home before dark.'

'But Marcia——'

'I told Marcia where we were going. The group are all here, and their girl-friends, and some other friends. We're going to have a barbecue on the beach.'

Caryn felt angry. 'You should have told me.'

'Why? Would you have come if you'd known?'

'No.'

'That's why I didn't tell you.'

'Oh, Dave!'

'No, that's not how you say it,' he teased. 'You say—oooh, Dave!' and he made it sound rather seductive, but Caryn was not in the mood for his humour.

St Gifford was smaller than Port Edward, just a collection of bungalows and cottages overlooking a narrow headland.

Its main industry was fishing, and because of its size it didn't attract a lot of tourists.

Dave drove down on to the narrow quay, and then turned up a gravelled slope to where a rambling bungalow overlooked a narrow stretch of sand cut off from the small harbour by the sea wall. The sound of beat music drifted from the back of the house, and Caryn turned to Dave as he climbed off the bike.

'Whose bungalow is this?'

'Greg's,' he answered, mentioning the name of one of the other members of Sweet Vibration. 'Does it matter who owns it? We all live here.'

'You do?'

'Well, sometimes,' he conceded goodnaturedly. 'Come on. I could sure use a beer!'

Caryn followed him reluctantly. She should have stuck to her original intention and not gone out with him, she thought ruefully. She had allowed her feelings about Tristan to catapult her into a situation she would dearly like to change.

They entered the bungalow through a wide porch, and thence along a passage which ran from front to back. They came out on a wide patio, and were immediately greeted like long-lost cousins. At least a dozen young people were spread about on li-los and padded loungers, and the music, louder here, came from the electronic equipment wired from a room inside. Refrigerated trolleys clinked with cans of beer, and the sickly scent of joss sticks was even evident outdoors.

'Hi, there!' The strongly American-flavoured drawl came from Allan Felix, the only transatlantic member of the group. He came to meet them with a slim blonde girl clinging to his shoulder, who cast slightly malicious looks at Caryn's vivid darkness.

'You know Al, don't you?' Dave asked, putting an arm round Caryn's shoulders and drawing her forward, but she shook him off and nodded at the American without enthusiasm.

'Say, you need a drink, I can see that,' Allan exclaimed, his drooping moustache giving character to his otherwise immature features. 'What'll it be? Beer? Lager? Coke?'

'Coke would be fine,' said Caryn, not really wanting anything and wanting his girl-friend's ire even less.

'That's Lindy,' Dave volunteered, as the blonde girl pouted after Allan, and Caryn gave him an indifferent stare.

Room was made for them on the loungers scattered about the paved area, and Caryn had to admire the sculptured stone tracery that bounded the patio, and the tumbling glory of honeysuckle and clematis that climbed about the lattice-work. The members of the group she knew by sight, of course, and one by one the others introduced themselves, most of the girls much less aggressive than Lindy. The uniform of the day seemed to be jeans and shirts, although one or two of the girls wore bikini bras underneath and had taken off their shirts.

Caryn guessed that most of the girls were younger than she was. The members of the group she was less sure about. Dave, she guessed, was in his late twenties, but Allan Felix and Greg Simons, and the drummer, Gene David, looked younger.

Allan returned with her Coke and as Dave was leaning over to talk to someone else, the American squatted down beside her.

'Don't I know you?' he asked, frowning, and she gave him an old-fashioned look.

'Techniques don't change, do they?' she countered. 'Why don't you try—*do you come here often?*'

Allan grinned. 'Point taken. But I meant it. You do remind me of somebody. I don't know why—something about the eyes, I guess.'

A thought suddenly struck her, and she felt contrite. 'You might have known my sister,' she ventured reluctantly. 'Loren?'

'Loren Stevens! Of course.' He knew who she meant at once. 'That's your sister? Hey—how is she?'

Caryn licked her lips. 'She's dead.'

'Dead?' He stared at her aghast. 'God, I'm sorry.' Lindy came to hang over his shoulder, and he glanced round at her impatiently. When she didn't take the hint, he elbowed her away, saying: 'Push off!' She went with a heightening of colour, and Caryn felt dreadful.

Feeling she had to say something, she asked: 'Er—did you know Loren well?' but he shook his head.

'Not very. She was always around the house, you know. I guess Dave knew her better than we did.'

'I see.' Caryn's eyes flickered reflectively over the other boy. Of course, Dave being a friend of Tristan's, he was bound to have seen more of her than any of the others.

'So . . .' Allan clearly wanted to change the subject. 'You're working for Tris now. How do you get on with Angel?'

Caryn was non-committal. 'I hardly know her. She's been away for the last month.'

'Cool!' he grinned. 'But keep away from Dave when she's around. She doesn't like competition.'

'Dave?' Caryn was surprised, and hearing his name mentioned he turned back to her.

'You called?' he asked teasingly, but she just coloured and shook her head and applied herself to her Coke.

In spite of the fact that there was a ready supply of food

and drink, and lively company, Caryn soon got bored. She wasn't too interested in drinking except when she was thirsty, and the scent of the joss sticks was not one she enjoyed. Everyone else drank pretty steadily throughout the afternoon and early evening, and by the time they began to set up the barbecue on the beach, they were all, with the possible exception of Lindy, slightly drunk. Caryn was not a prude, but she deplored their behaviour, and the idea of riding back to Port Edward on the back of Dave's bike filled her with misgivings. He ought not to be driving anywhere, and she wished she had suggested coming in her car. But then she had not known their destination, or that they were staying all evening.

She went into the bungalow once to use the bathroom, and wondered if there was a telephone. Perhaps if she rang Druid's Fleet and asked Marcia to come and get her? The housekeeper knew how to drive, and there was a Mini that she used to go shopping in Carmarthen. Maybe if she just told her what was going on she would feel better.

She met Lindy in the hall as she came out of the bathroom, and on impulse, she asked her if there was a telephone.

'Why d'you wanna know?' she demanded sulkily, and Caryn sighed.

'I want to ring home—that is, to the place where I live.'

'Why?'

'I'd like to leave,' declared Caryn, taking the chance that as Lindy had no love for her she might be glad to see the back of her.

'You wanna leave?' Lindy looked suspicious. 'You and who else?'

'Only me,' exclaimed Caryn, in a low tone, aware that any

minute one of the others could come upon them. 'Please. Is there a phone?'

'Sure. There's one in there,' replied Lindy, gesturing with her thumb towards a door to one side of the front porch, and thanking her, Caryn hurried towards it.

The room she entered was a living room, and judging from the smell of tobacco smoke it was seldom aired. But sure enough, there was a telephone by the couch, and she closed the door and went eagerly towards it.

It took her a few seconds to find the code for Port Edward, but she knew Tristan's number by heart, and she dialled the figures with trembling fingers. It seemed to ring for an age before anyone answered it, and when the receiver was lifted, the voice that gave the number was masculine.

She was silent for a moment, and he repeated the number, and with bated breath, she said: '*Tristan!* Tristan, is that you?'

'Caryn?' He sounded surprised. Then, more sharply: 'Is something wrong?'

Caryn's brain worked furiously. Why was Tristan there? Was he alone? Or was Melanie Forbes with him?

'I—why—no,' she answered him now, before adding quickly: 'Could I speak to Marcia, please?'

'Marcia?' His voice had cooled perceptibly. 'Caryn, where are you?'

'Oh, please, I don't have much time . . .'

Caryn could hear voices in the hall outside, and she was terrified someone would come in and ask her what the hell she thought she was doing.

'*Caryn!*' Her name grated now. 'Where are you? I want to know.'

'Didn't Marcia explain?'

'Marcia wrote a note that told me only that Dave was

taking you out for a meal, and then to the pictures in Carmarthen.'

'Oh, lord!'

Her troubled words were audible to him, and she heard his baffled oath. 'If you don't tell me where you are, I warn you, when you get back here——'

'I'm at a place called St Gifford,' she confessed hastily.

'St Gifford!' She sensed his anger now. 'At Greg Simons' place?'

'Yes . . .'

'God Almighty! What are you doing there?'

'I—I didn't know where we were going,' she began, but he cut her off.

'I'll be there in a little under an hour!' he snapped harshly, and the phone went dead.

She was emerging from the living room when she saw Dave coming looking for her. 'What have you been doing?' he exclaimed, his eyes moving past her to the living room door, and she made an awkward gesture.

'I've just been looking around,' she replied offhandedly, and although he looked suspicious for a moment, he had other things on his mind.

'Well, come on,' he urged. 'We've got the barbecue going, and Greg wants to know how you like your steak.'

Caryn accompanied him across the patio and down the rocky steps to the beach. It was gritty sand, and scratched her toes, but she kept her discomfort to herself, and sat on one end of a wooden seat, knees drawn up, wondering in an agony of apprehension what Tristan would do. The others had set a transistor going and were making hilarious attempts at dancing on the sand, but when Dave tried to persuade her to join them, she shook her head, pretending she was watching Greg cook the steaks.

Lindy sidled across to her, and quirked an eyebrow. 'Well?' she demanded. 'Did you find it?'

Caryn frowned at her, wishing she would keep her voice down, but Allan overhearing them asked: 'Find it? Find what?'

'The loo, stupid!' replied Lindy shortly, and Caryn breathed more freely.

The charcoal got too hot and the first lot of steaks blackened unappetisingly. Another batch were rescued from the kitchen and Caryn glanced surreptitiously at her watch. It was after eight o'clock. How much longer was Tristan going to be? She found she was waiting for his arrival with almost desperate anticipation.

Dave came back to her, tailed by a redhead who had shed her shirt and jeans to reveal a black bikini. 'Come on,' he said, raising the can of beer he carried to his lips. 'You ain't havin' any fun!'

Caryn ignored him, and suddenly his hand shot out and caught a handful of her hair. 'Don't you turn your back on me!' he told her angrily, and she winced as her scalp tingled from the fierceness of his hold on her hair.

'Leave her be!' The redhead gazed up at him impatiently. 'Come'n, dance with me.'

Dave released Caryn's hair, but his mouth was aggressive. 'What is it with you?' he demanded. 'Loren used not to be so standoffish.'

Caryn stared at him contemptuously, and as she did so, she heard Allan give a low whistle. 'Look who's here! The boss man himself.'

Both Dave and Caryn turned to see Tristan coming down the steps, lean and disturbingly familiar in dark blue corded pants and a matching shirt. But he was not alone. A slender reed of a girl was with him, her honey-brown hair secured back from her face with an orange velvet band. Her dress was orange too, long and silky, and obviously unsuitable for a barbecue on the beach. Caryn knew who she was at once. Melanie Forbes, in the flesh.

Dave cast a curious look in Caryn's direction as he went to greet the newcomers. 'You're just in time,' he declared expansively, gesturing towards the barbecue. 'Steaks for everyone!'

'Not for me, darling!' Melanie obviously knew the group. 'Steaks are much too fattening!'

Tristan's eyes had sought and found Caryn's, but she didn't move. She couldn't help it, but she resented the fact that he had brought his girl-friend with him. Why couldn't he have come alone? Wasn't it embarrassing enough?

'So what gives?' asked Greg, going to join them, but before Tristan could explain, Melanie exclaimed:

'Where's Tris's secretary? That's why we're here. Apparently she wants to go home!'

Caryn's face went first scarlet, then white, as they all turned to look at her. She had never felt so small in her life, and she stared down miserably at her toes.

'It's my fault.' She heard Tristan's voice through the mists of agonised embarrassment. 'I told Caryn I was taking her back,' he stated calmly, although as she ventured to look at him she saw different emotions smouldering in the depths of the tawny eyes. 'She rang Marcia to tell her she'd be late, and I'm afraid I blew my top.'

Only Dave appeared to doubt this. 'Caryn rang Marcia?' he echoed. 'She didn't tell me.'

'Is there any reason why she should?' enquired Tristan evenly, and suddenly another note had entered the proceedings.

'Oh, come on, darling!' Melanie tugged at Tristan's arm.

'For goodness' sake, where is she? Then we can go. You
promised we'd go to the Donnellys' later.'

Caryn got up off the bench and came towards them.
'I'm here,' she said clearly, and saw the disparaging look
Melanie cast in her direction. She guessed she did deserve
it at that. She hadn't combed her hair since riding the motor-
bike, and it tangled curls framed her face like a dark halo.
Her make-up was non-existent, but the dusky tan of her
skin needed little in the way of cosmetics, if she had but
known it.

Tristan indicated that she should precede them up the
steps, and with an apologetic farewell to the others, Caryn
went ahead. She went through the house and out through
the porch, stopping beside the grey Mercedes almost reluctantly.

Tristan passed Melanie and swung open the rear passenger
door. He looked at Caryn and her lids lowered mutinously
as she obediently got into the back of the car. He slammed
the door behind her, and then smiled his apology at Melanie
for keeping her waiting.

'I didn't introduce you,' he said, as he levered himself
behind the wheel, beside the other girl. 'Caryn, this is
Melanie; Melanie—Caryn.'

Melanie barely glanced round at the third passenger, but
pulled a face at Tristan. 'Honestly, darling,' she said, as they
pulled away, 'was it necessary to speak to Dave like that? In
front of all his friends?'

Tristan made no answer, and she tried again: 'Don't you
think this whole thing is rather silly? I mean, it's obvious
Miss—Miss——'

'Stevens,' supplied Caryn stiffly, and was rewarded by a
slight smile.

'—Stevens, then; it's obvious Miss Stevens is perfectly old enough to take care of herself!'

'Just mind your own business, will you, Melanie?' he suggested, showing none of the charm which Caryn knew he could exert when he chose, and the girl beside him turned to stare sulkily out of the window.

But by the time they reached Druid's Fleet she had come round again, and was talking quite animatedly about some friends called Beth and Peter, whose party she wanted them to attend later.

Tristan turned between the gates of the drive and let the Mercedes coast down to the door. At once Caryn thrust open her door and got out, but by the time she had circled the car to the porch, he was beside her.

'I want to talk to you,' he said quietly, and she glanced back at Melanie, still in the car.

'Not now,' she protested pointedly, but he nodded his head.

'Right now.'

'But Melanie——'

'Leave Melanie to me,' he stated grimly, and thrust open the door into the hall.

Caryn preceded him inside and stood looking at him uncertainly. It was worse than suffering Laurence's disapproval, she thought, and she resented his attitude. She hadn't asked him to come and fetch her. He had taken that decision. And yet he seemed to be blaming her for what happened.

'I'm sorry,' she said, deciding to take the bull by the horns. 'I've spoiled your evening.'

'You have a habit of doing that,' he retorted, pushing the door to behind them, but not securing it. 'Whatever possessed you to go off with O'Hara?'

'I didn't go off with O'Hara! I've told you, I thought we were just going for a ride.'

He gave her a narrow look. 'Yet Marcia maintains that he told her he was taking you to the cinema.'

'I can't help that.'

'You deny you knew you were going to the cinema?'

'I? Deny it?' She stared indignantly at him. 'Why should I deny it? I'm not a liar.'

'Aren't you?'

Caryn stared at him in silence for a few moments, her mouth working impotently, and then without another word she turned and ran up the stairs and along the corridor to her room.

She leant back against the closed door, trying to still the racing of her heart, and then gasped when it was suddenly propelled inward. Tristan stood just inside the door, and when she would have evaded him, he caught her shoulder and pressed the door closed again with her against it.

'Wh-what do you think you're doing?' she blurted. 'This is my room!' but her words made no difference to the metallic hardness of his eyes.

'I said I wanted to talk to you, and if we have to do it here, that's okay by me,' he stated, one hand on either side of her now, imprisoning her against the glossy panels of the door. 'Do you realise this is the second time in as many weeks that you've disrupted my life?'

'I've told you I'm sorry. What more can I say?'

'What exactly did Dave say to you?'

'Does it matter?'

'I think so.'

She sighed, shifting restively. 'He said—how would I like to go for a ride!'

'And you went—just like that?'

'No.' Caryn denied it, and then qualified the negation by adding: 'Why shouldn't I, anyway?'

'You're asking me that? After tonight's little fiasco?'

She bent her head. 'They didn't do anything . . .'

'I see.' His voice was incisive. 'So you'd have stayed there if I hadn't come to fetch you?'

'I didn't have much choice, did I?'

He straightened, his arms falling to his sides. 'I can see I'm wasting my time in talking to you. I foolishly imagined your phone call was a cry for help!'

He moved away from her, and at once she felt a heel. Her motive for ringing Marcia had been one of distress, and he had not been mistaken in recognising that note of panic in her voice.

'I'd better go,' he said, running an exploring hand over the buttons of his shirt, checking that they were all in place. One had come unloosened in his exchange with Caryn, and his fingers moved to fasten it while she watched feeling miserable. But when the button stubbornly refused to go into its hole, she stepped forward and said jerkily: 'Let me!'

Her nails brushed his chest as she went to fasten the button, scraping against the fine covering of sun-bleached hair that curled upon itself. It made what she was doing that much more intimate somehow, and her gaze darted up to his almost apologetically.

'You should have told me to mind my own business,' he said as she secured the button, and much against her will her fingers lingered against the silken feel of his shirt, wanting to stay his departure.

'You—you were right,' she confessed in a low voice. 'I did want to get away from there. They—they were drinking too much, and—and I was afraid that Dave might—might——'

'—get the wrong idea?' he finished softly, and she nodded.

'I really didn't know where he was taking me, and when I found out . . .'

'You panicked?'

'Something like that.'

'Oh, Caryn!' The urgency in his voice caused her to look up at him, but he put her away from him and went towards the door. 'I'll have Marcia bring you up a tray,' he added more gently, and she realised he was feeling sorry for her now.

Perversely, this knowledge did not please her. She didn't want his sympathy, she thought with a return of anger. She didn't want him going back to Melanie and telling her what a fool Dave had made of her. Melanie would like that, she decided maliciously, without possessing a shred of proof to justify her belief.

'Don't bother,' she retorted now as he reached for the handle. 'I'll speak to Marcia myself. You look after Melanie. I'm sure she'll reward you more than adequately for anything you do for her.'

Tristan stiffened. 'What do you mean by that?'

'Nothing.' Caryn moved her shoulders offhandedly. 'You'd better hurry. I don't suppose she likes being kept waiting any more than you do.'

'You little bitch!' He stared at her furiously. 'You know damn all about it!'

Caryn shrugged. 'Dave told me who her daddy was.'

'Oh, did he?' Tristan took a step towards her. 'When was this? Before or after the joyride?'

Caryn scuffed her toe. 'Does it matter?'

'It might. If I thought you were jealous—and that was why you chose to go out with O'Hara!'

'*Jealous!*' Caryn's laugh was cracked. 'You must be joking!'

'Must I?' He didn't look convinced.

'Oh, go to hell!' she declared shortly, and turned her back on him.

She heard his angry ejaculation, and then hard hands gripped her arms, jerking her back against him. For several seconds he just held her there, imprisoned against him, and then, when she started to struggle, he twisted her round and covered her mouth with his own.

His lips bruised hers, but when she tried to speak against him her parting lips only made his kiss that much more intimate. Gradually weakness took the place of aggression. In a short time she was kissing him back, which was all the more degrading when she knew his strongest emotion at that moment was anger.

He was wanting to hurt her but, in spite of himself, she felt the moment when her closeness began to arouse him against his will. The throbbing pressure that surged between them was something she had never felt before, and a low groan escaped him as he realised what was happening.

'*God!*' he muttered thickly, staring down at her, his hands on her shoulders inside the unbuttoned neckline of her shirt, and then, with an obvious effort, he dragged himself away from her and made it to the door.

'Tris . . .' she whispered huskily, gazing after him, but the door slammed hollowly behind him.

CHAPTER EIGHT

She had gone into the bathroom to rinse her hot face in cold water when someone knocked at her bedroom door. Guessing it might be Miss Trewen, Caryn hastily fastened her shirt across her breasts as she walked back into the bedroom. But before she had time to call: 'Who is it?' her door opened and Melanie appeared.

Caryn was so astounded to see the other girl, her first reaction was one of guilt, and she could feel the revealing colour staining her cheeks.

'Did you want something?' she asked, trying to behave normally, and Melanie regarded her without liking.

'Is Tristan here?' she asked, looking about her, and Caryn pushed her hands into her hip pockets to hide their trembling.

'Tris—Mr Ross?' she asked unevenly. 'Why, no!'

'But he was with you a few minutes ago, wasn't he?' exclaimed Melanie impatiently. 'I heard you arguing downstairs when I was waiting in the car.'

Caryn absorbed this, and then shook her head. 'I'm afraid I don't know where he is now.' That at least was true!

'Huh!' Melanie took another look around the bedroom. Then she leaned on the door-knob and said: 'This is a nice room, isn't it? Much nicer than mine, actually.' As Caryn didn't know what to say to that, she remained silent, and Melanie continued: 'How long have you been here? I can't remember when it was Tristan said he employed you.'

Her meaning was obvious. She wanted to make their respective positions clear right from the outset, and Caryn wondered why she wanted to argue with her. It was unlikely that their paths would cross very often—unless Tristan married her.

But that eventuality she forced aside, along with her own attraction towards him, and the disturbing realisation that if she stayed here, sooner or later she might find herself as helpless in his hands as Loren had been.

All the same, she wondered where he had gone when he left her, and the possible solution brought another wave of colour into her cheeks.

'I—I've been here nearly six weeks,' she said now, suddenly becoming aware that Melanie was getting impatient, and the other girl frowned.

'That long? Don't you find it rather lonely here, with only Marcia for company?'

'You're forgetting the child and his nurse, Melanie,' Tristan remarked behind her, and she swung round to gaze at him in teasing disapproval.

'So there you are!' she exclaimed, and hearing the faint edge to her voice, Caryn decided her irritation was not all pretence. 'Where have you been?'

Tristan came into view, changed now into cream suede slacks and a matching fine wool jerkin. 'I was—hot,' he explained, his eyes flickering coldly over Caryn before melting into Melanie's. 'I took a quick shower. Forgive me.'

Melanie's fingers slid between his and gripped his palm. 'Can we go to the Donnellys' now?' she asked, moving so that her small breasts brushed his arm, and Caryn looked away.

'I don't see why not,' he agreed mildly, and with a fleeting glance in Caryn's direction, he drew Melanie outside and closed the door.

Caryn slept badly. She blamed it on the salmon Marcia had

prepared for supper, but in all honesty she knew her problems were mental rather than physical. After Tristan and Melanie had left, she too had taken a shower, but instead of cooling her blood it had quickened it, and she lay there in the moonlit shadows wondering how much longer it would be before Tristan and his girl-friend returned from their party. At three o'clock she fell into an uneasy slumber from which she was awakened some time later by the sound of a closing door. Guessing her employer was home, she expelled her breath on a long sigh, but although she waited until the dawn light was colouring the eastern sky, she heard no sound of a second door closing.

In consequence she overslept, and it was after nine before the brightness of her room alerted her to the fact that it was Friday and her employer might well be waiting for her to take dictation.

She forwent her shower and washed and dressed quickly in a navy blue shirtwaister, with elbow-length sleeves. She seldom wore tights these days, but today she put some on, and a pair of heeled shoes instead of her sandals.

She was hurrying down the split-level hall to the study when she encountered Marcia coming from the opposite direction. They both stopped, and Caryn quickly asked if Tristan was waiting for her, but Marcia merely shook her head. Smiling, she put her palms together and placed them against her bent cheek, signifying as clearly as any words that their employer was still in bed.

Caryn's shoulders sagged. 'I thought he might be waiting for me.' She gave a rueful smile. 'I overslept, too.'

Marcia shook her head, and taking the girl's arm, drew her back along the hall and through the door that led to the kitchen. Miming raising a cup to her lips, Marcia raised her eyebrows, and Caryn nodded.

'Yes,' she said, 'I would like some coffee. And some toast, too, if it's not too much trouble.'

Miss Trewen came in as Caryn was finishing her breakfast, carrying the baby. At almost five months, he could hold his head quite erect, and responded with a gurgling smile to anyone's attention.

Immediately Caryn got up to take him from the nurse, and Miss Trewen surrendered him gladly.

'He's been awake half the night,' she exclaimed, lifting the lid of the coffee pot anticipatorily. 'Is there another cup, do you think?'

Caryn pushed Tristan's fingers out of her mouth, and giggled as he tangled them in her hair. 'Have you been a naughty boy?' she exclaimed, finding an escape from her own problems in playing with him, and he blew bubbles in her face.

'Mr Ross has a guest staying, did you know?' the nurse asked, after Marcia had provided her with a fresh pot of coffee, and Caryn nodded, glad of the distraction of the child to hide her real feelings.

'I—met her last night,' she answered, pushing her face close to Tristan's, and as she did so she was struck by a fleeting glimpse of familiarity. It was gone in a second, but the impression lingered, teasing her memory by its lack of definition. She frowned into the baby's eyes, seeking to rediscover that trace of identity, and turned to the door almost apprehensively when it unexpectedly opened.

It was Tristan who came in, looking much the worse for his late night. His deep-set eyes were pouched and lacklustre, and deep lines were etched beside his mouth. He was wearing a navy towelling robe over white silk pyjama trousers, and it was the first time Caryn had seen him without his day clothes. In consequence, her eyes lingered on him longer than was necessary and eventually encountered the chilling depths of his. Then he switched his attention to the baby in her arms, and she felt desperately vulnerable at that moment. After all, the child's future depended on her maintaining a working relationship with this man, and last night she had done much to destroy it.

He seemed surprised to find the three women of his household all together, and Miss Trewen immediately began to make excuses for being there.

'Tristan's beginning to cut a tooth, Mr Ross,' she exclaimed apologetically, 'and I've had quite a wakeful night.'

The smile he gave her was wry. 'I've had one of those myself, Miss Trewen,' he assured her, his words cutting through Caryn's defences without effort. 'Don't hurry away on my account. Marcia, do we have any magnesia?' Marcia gave him a look of disapproval, and his response was good-natured. 'I know, I know—I drink too much. But do we have any?'

Caryn felt Miss Trewen beside her and would have surrendered the baby to her, only Tristan chose that moment to come across himself and speak to the child. It necessitated him coming close to Caryn, and the wide bottoms of his pyjama trousers actually brushed her ankles. He allowed his namesake to grasp one of his fingers, and judging from the way the baby responded to him it was not the first time he had spoken to him. Then, under cover of the baby's gurgling, Tristan's eyes moved to Caryn, and he said cynically:

'And you said babies didn't interest you!'

'This baby does,' she murmured huskily, and his lips curled.

'I wonder. Perhaps I should be flattered at the attention you pay—*my* son!'

Caryn glanced at Miss Trewen in an agonised way, but

fortunately she was looking the other way and Tristan's words had been so low as to be scarcely audible even to her. Nevertheless, she moved away from him, taking the baby out of reach of his fingers and arousing a cry of protest because of that. But at least it brought Miss Trewen's attention back to her charge, and she lifted him out of Caryn's arms with a murmur of reproval.

'Come along,' she said. 'It's time for our nap, isn't it?'

Marcia set a bottle of magnesia down on the table with a force that made the coffee cups rattle, and Miss Trewen disappeared as Marcia began to remonstrate with her employer by means of hand signals.

Tristan glanced round at Caryn, and his expression was mocking. 'You should enjoy this,' he drawled. 'Marcia is telling me what a fool I am.'

Caryn coloured. 'I'll go along to the study, Mr Ross,' she stated, moving towards the door, and he shrugged his acquiescence. 'Will you be working this morning?'

Tristan swallowed some of the magnesia from a spoon, and grimaced expressively. Then he wiped his mouth with the back of his hand, and regarded her sourly.

'You can have the next few days off,' he declared at last. 'Melanie's father will be joining us here for the weekend, and although some of our talk will be business, you don't need to be involved.'

'I see.' Caryn felt suddenly flat. 'But I don't mind working.'

Tristan's nostrils flared. 'I've told you—take some time off.' He paused. 'Go to London, why don't you? See that friend of yours in Bloomsbury.'

'Laura?' Caryn caught her lower lip between her teeth, feeling suddenly guilty. Apart from a letter after they had arrived in Port Edward she had not corresponded with

Laura, and she realised with a pang that her time for having the baby must be getting very near.

'What's the matter?' Seemingly he could ignore Marcia's unobtrusive presence. 'I thought you'd welcome the chance to get away from here for a few days.'

Caryn caught her breath. 'Per-perhaps I would.' She smoothed her moist palms down the skirt of her dress. 'When do you want me to leave?'

'When do I——' He broke off abruptly, his face contorted with sudden anger, and his hands sought the corded tie of his bathrobe. 'I think I'd better get dressed. I'll speak to you in the study in fifteen minutes, Miss Stevens!'

Alone with Marcia, she shifted awkwardly, but the housekeeper just pulled a sympathetic face and Caryn felt a surge of affection for the other woman. Without Tristan's disruptive presence, Druid's Fleet had become a real home to her, and it was that much more painful to feel she was being excluded from it.

In the study, she tidied her desk, filed away the copies of the report she had been typing the day before, and checked that all the dictaphone tapes were stacked in their box. Then she moved to Tristan's desk, gathering up his pens and slotting them back into their holder. She had seated herself in his chair to put some files back in a lower drawer when the door opened and he came in. Immediately, her instinct was to spring to her feet and return to her own desk, but something, some rebellious spirit kept her where she was.

He had had a shower, and the thick smoothness of his hair lay like wet silk against his head. His brown velvet jerkin matched the colour of his denims, and their narrowness accentuated the lean strength of his hips and the powerful muscles between.

He closed the door and leaned back against it for a

moment before straightening and walking towards her. He halted before the desk, folding his arms, feet apart, and said: 'How does it feel?'

Caryn's palms moulded the leather seat. 'Very—comfortable.'

'You think so?' There was no trace of humour in his face, and she felt uncomfortable.

'Why did you want to speak to me?' she prompted, but he continued to look down at her with such a brooding expression that she was forced to take action. Pushing back the chair, she got to her feet and came round the desk, only to find he had stepped into her path.

'Did you sleep well?' he demanded unexpectedly, and she gulped.

'Did I sleep well?' she echoed. 'What's that to you?'

'I'd like to know whether you were able to lay your head on the pillow and coax the mists of Morpheus after what you did to me!' he declared savagely. 'I like to know what I'm dealing with! Whether the *lady* has a conscience!'

Caryn trembled. 'Mr Ross,' she began unsteadily, 'I'd like to apologise for—for what I said last ni——'

'Like hell you would!' His hands descended on her shoulders, cruelly penetrating. 'What's caused this sudden change of heart, I wonder?' He frowned. 'Why should you apologise to me? It's not in character. Unless . . .' His eyes narrowed. 'Unless you're afraid I'll turn you—and junior—out!'

'All right!' She almost shouted the words at him. 'All right. That's the truth! You hold us both in the palm of your hand, don't you? Well, there's nothing I can do about that, not right now, and if I have to grovel—well, I guess I'll do that too!' She paused only long enough to take a breath. 'But don't think you can make me feel guilty for the way you feel this morning, because you can't! I didn't do anything to you that a couple of hours spent with Melanie Forbes wouldn't put right, and you spent more than a couple of hours with her, didn't you? In fact, I wouldn't be surprised if you spent the whole night with her! It's such a saving on bed-linen, isn't it?' she flung at him.

There was an awful silence after that, only broken by the steady ticking of the clock on the mantelshelf, and the tortured sound of her breathing. Caryn's spirits plummeted. Oh God! she thought. She had really done it now! How on earth could she justify an accusation like that?

His hands fell from her shoulders and he looked down at them as if they might have been contaminated. 'That's what you think, is it?' he asked expressionlessly, and her nerves jangled discordantly. 'Would you have thought better of me if I had slept with you?'

Caryn's throat contracted. 'No——'

'But you knew what you'd done,' he persisted. 'Why shouldn't I have—relieved my frustrations with someone else?'

Caryn's breath caught and held. 'Is that your excuse?' she choked, and his lips twisted.

'According to your opinion of me, I don't need an excuse. What are you afraid of, Caryn? That I might make Melanie pregnant, too? And marry her?'

Caryn couldn't take any more of this. 'If you want me out of the house for the weekend, then I'll go,' she stated tightly, and saw the contempt in his eyes.

'Oh, yes,' he said bitterly, 'I want you out of the house for the weekend. But not for the reasons you think. Now, get the hell out of here before I do something to cripple that sordid little mind of yours!'

She was reaching for the door handle when Melanie's face appeared coyly round the corner of the panelling. Her expression changed sharply when she saw Caryn, and then dimpled once more when she glimpsed Tristan by the desk.

'Oh, you are here, darling!' she exclaimed, widening the aperture to reveal a pink flowered cotton wrapper that moulded her small pointed breasts. 'I thought that was what Marcia was trying to tell me. Honestly, darling, I don't know how you stand having her about the place—not being able to take any messages, or answer the phone.'

'Marcia suits me,' he stated grimly, and Caryn recognised the note of thinly-veiled anger in his voice if Melanie didn't.

'I know you feel responsible for her, darling,' she went on, unwittingly provoking, 'but it wasn't your fault that her husband and her baby were slaughtered by those crazy African tribesmen——'

'Leave it, Melanie!'

As in the car the evening before, he silenced her with a curt rejoinder, and Melanie's cheeks bloomed with unbecoming colour. Caryn decided it was time she was gone, and with a muffled word of apology, she brushed past the other girl and walked quickly up the corridor.

But in her room her shoulders sagged weakly. Considering it was barely ten o'clock, it had been a gruelling day so far. But at least Melanie's careless words had revealed a little of Marcia's background, and imagining the horrifying scenes she must have witnessed, Caryn felt an overwhelming sense of pity for her. How she came to be working for Tristan, she could only guess, but reluctantly she had to concede that giving the woman a home and a purpose in life was the kind of thing he would do.

After packing her case, she went along to the nursery to tell Miss Trewen she was going away for the weekend. The nurse was busy tidying the room after putting Tristan down for his morning sleep, but she smiled when Caryn came in.

'I wanted to have a private word with you, Miss Stevens,' she said, and Caryn's already taut nerves stretched.

'You did?'

'Yes.' Miss Trewen rummaged in her capacious handbag and came out with a letter. 'This came this morning. It's from an old college friend of mine. I wrote to her soon after we came here. She lives in Aberystwyth, you see, and I hoped she might suggest a meeting.'

Caryn tensed as she guessed what was coming. 'And she has?'

'She wants me to spend a day with her, actually,' admitted Miss Trewen eagerly. 'Do you think Sunday would be all right?'

'Sunday?' Caryn swallowed with difficulty. 'Well . . .'

'I'm sure Mr Ross won't mind. I mean, it has been six weeks . . .'

'Oh, yes, indeed.' Caryn forced a faint smile. 'You're—entitled to it, naturally.' She bit her lip. 'I—yes, Sunday would be fine.'

'Oh, good. I thought I would ring her this afternoon, if it was all right.'

Caryn nodded. 'As a matter of fact, I—er—I'm going away myself today.'

'You are?' Miss Trewen looked surprised. 'Well, well. Two minds with but a single thought.'

'Yes.' Caryn made a casual movement of her shoulders. 'I'd better be going.'

'You'll be back tonight?'

'Er—no. Tomorrow.'

'Tomorrow! I see. Mr Ross doesn't need you.'

'It was his idea, actually,' Caryn confessed reluctantly, and the nurse looked concerned.

'Oh, dear! Am I spoiling your weekend?'

'Heavens, no!' Caryn wondered why the idea of coming back a day earlier than expected filled her with relief. One day less for Tristan to decide he could do without her, she pondered uneasily, and walked towards the door. 'See you tomorrow evening, then.'

Miss Trewen nodded. 'Have a good time,' she urged, and Caryn swallowed back the impulse to admit that she didn't really want to go at all.

CHAPTER NINE

She felt guilty about her lack of enthusiasm when she met Laura. The other girl was obviously so delighted to see her, and exclaimed at once how well Caryn was looking.

'How lucky you are, living by the sea!' she said enviously, and studying Laura's heated face and swollen ankles, Caryn wondered how she could ever have thought that London was a suitable place to bring up a family.

'There are advantages,' she admitted now, coming into Laura's flat which, in spite of its size, was always so beautifully clean. 'Where's Bob?'

'Where do you think?' Laura pulled a face. 'Working.' She sighed. 'If only he could get a job out of the city, so we could buy a house in the country! But on his salary . . .'

She trudged into the kitchen to put on the kettle, and Caryn wandered to the window. Outside the chimneypots of London were no substitute for the wide reaches of the estuary, and the traffic that hooted two floors below was an assault to ears attuned to the gentler sounds of the river.

Laura came back into the room and flopped down into a chair. 'Three more weeks of this!' she declared, fanning herself with a newspaper. 'I don't know if I can stand it.'

Caryn looked at her sympathetically. 'How do you manage the stairs?'

'I don't. Except when I have to attend the clinic. Bob does all the shopping for us, and I'm stuck up here from dawn till dusk waiting for him to come home.'

'But what about your mother?' exclaimed Caryn, remembering the rather sour-faced woman who had been an occasional visitor at the flat, but Laura shook her head.

'She never got on with Bob, you know that. And—well, after you left there was an awful row one evening about me being here alone all the time, with no one to turn to if the baby should come early.'

'But what about the other flat?'

'It hasn't been let yet. I've heard that the landlady's daughter is going to take it when she gets married, in October. But I don't know if that's true or not.'

'Oh, Laura!' Caryn felt really worried about her friend now. 'Your mother's right, you know. You should have someone you could call on.'

'Who do you suggest? Mr Sugden? Or that awful Miss Peel?'

Caryn frowned. 'Well, Mr Sugden is at work all day himself,' she said reflectively, understanding Laura's reluctance to speak to him. Word had it that he was a divorcee, but privately they both thought he was rather a peculiar fellow, in more ways than one. Miss Peel was another matter. Only about ten years older than Caryn, she had the first floor front, and although she had no obvious means of support, she never seemed short of gentlemen callers. Neither of them were what Caryn would have termed 'approachable' and her concern for her friend increased.

'Well,' she said now, seeing how depressed Laura was beginning to look, 'if you've got somewhere I can sleep, I can stay until tomorrow, and I insist on doing the weekend's shopping as I'm here.'

'Oh, Caryn!'

To her consternation, she saw a tear trickling down Laura's cheek, but with a determination she was far from feeling, she ignored it, and marching into the kitchen made the tea. By the time she came back, Laura had herself in control again, and Caryn managed to divert her by telling her how baby Tristan was developing, and describing in ludicrous detail her own experiences at the hands of Sweet Vibration. She omitted all references to Tristan Ross, however, and the small voice inside her that monitored her true feelings chided her for being a coward.

The two days went remarkably quickly. Going to the stores for Laura, Caryn realised how out of touch with the prices of things she had become, and how soon she had adapted to her new way of life. It was dangerous, she reflected, climbing the stairs to the flat again. Sooner or later, the position with Tristan was going to become untenable, and she would find it doubly hard to take up her old life if she let all the threads of it escape her. She tried not to think what she would do if he did decide to fire her. Or indeed how baby Tristan would fare without his father's patronage . . .

Laura's husband, Bob, was grateful for her visit.

'Laura gets few visitors these days,' he told her, when his wife was out of the room. 'I worry about her, but what can I do? Someone has to earn the bread.'

'I wish there was something I could do,' confessed Caryn with a sigh. 'I feel a heel for abandoning her right at the time the baby's due.'

Bob nodded, then glancing surreptitiously behind him, he whispered: 'Look, don't say anything to her, will you, but I'm going for an interview next week, with Area-South Television. If I get the job, we may just be able to afford a house, out near the studios at Willesden.'

'Oh, Bob!' Caryn's face flushed with pleasure. 'That would be marvellous!'

'I know.' He hunched his shoulders. 'The only thing is, as I've had no experience in television, my chances are practically nil!'

Caryn's excitement evaporated. 'And is it compulsory? Having experience, I mean?'

'No. But if a guy goes along who has experience—well, I guess I'm out of the running.'

Caryn frowned, thinking hard. Area-South Television. Wasn't that the company Melanie's father controlled? Her brain ran on. Maybe it wasn't entirely ethical to think the way she was doing, but Bob and Laura deserved a break. If the other applicants were already working in television, the chances were they were already earning twice as much as Bob, and therefore not half so desperate. But, and this was the crunch, how could she expect Melanie to help her? The girl didn't even like her, and although the feeling was mutual, Melanie had had the added insult of Tristan setting her down twice in Caryn's presence.

Tristan!

Of course. He was the logical person to ask. But how could she ask him for anything after the way she had behaved?

Bob, who had been watching the play of emotions across her expressive face, now leaned towards her. 'Caryn,' he said, and she looked at him questioningly. 'Look, I don't like putting this to you, but—well, I happen to know Tristan Ross has shares in Area-South. You couldn't see your way clear to—putting in a word for me, could you?'

Caryn stared at him. 'Oh, Bob——'

'I know, it's a bloody cheek. But I'm desperate, Caryn. And there's no one else can help us but you.'

Hearing it put like that, Caryn was in an impossible position. 'But I don't know Mr Ross that well,' she protested.

'You live in his house, don't you? You work for him. I know you're good at your job. Surely as a favour to his secretary—to his almost sister-in-law——'

'Bob, Tristan Ross still denies that the child is his.'

Bob sighed. 'Okay, okay.' He rose abruptly to his feet. 'Sorry I asked.'

'Don't be.' Caryn felt terrible. 'Look, I'll see what I can do.'

Parting from Laura was upsetting. The other girl wept, and Caryn left the flat feeling utterly miserable. But it wasn't her fault! she told herself impatiently. The trouble was, she felt guilty on several counts.

It was quite late in the evening when she arrived back at Druid's Fleet, and Marcia met her with the news that Mr Ross had taken his guests out for the evening.

'Did he know you were coming back?' she scribbled on her pad, and Caryn frowned.

'Didn't Miss Trewen explain?' she asked, and when Marcia looked blank, added: 'She's going to Aberystwyth tomorrow, to spend the day with some college friend of hers. She asked me if I would look after Tristan.'

Marcia acknowledged this with a frown. Then she nodded, and wrote again: 'I don't think Sir George is aware there's a baby in the house, but I know Melanie resents what she thinks is the unfair favouritism shown to Loren's child.'

Caryn sighed. 'Then maybe I'd better make myself scarce as well. I shouldn't like to cause any more trouble.'

Marcia gave her a wry look, and she coloured shamefacedly. 'Well! I didn't ask to come here!'

Marcia wrote again: 'Have you ever considered that it might not be Mr Ross's child?' and Caryn looked at her disappointedly.

'Don't you believe me?' she exclaimed, and Marcia bent her head to the pad.

'I think Loren needed love—a man's love—very badly. When Mr Ross wouldn't give it to her, she went elsewhere.'

Caryn gasped. 'I thought you were my friend!' she cried. She turned blindly for the door. 'Why else would a man take on the financial responsibilities for a child?' she demanded hotly, but Tristan's words: *'Christian charity!'* echoed hollowly in her head.

Miss Trewen woke her on Sunday morning, coming into her room at half past seven and arousing her from the predawn slumber she had only just managed to achieve.

'Sorry to disturb you,' the nurse whispered, with a teasing smile, as Caryn scrambled up, dragging the sheets around her chin. 'But my taxi's coming at half past eight, and I thought I ought to brief you before I left.'

Caryn blinked. 'Of course.' She shook her head, trying to think coherently. 'What do you want me to do?'

'I should say get dressed first,' murmured Miss Trewen, obviously in high spirits, and Caryn nodded and slid her legs over the edge of the mattress.

A cold shower did wonders for her concentration, and by the time she appeared in the nursery, casually attired in jeans and sweater, Miss Trewen had Tristan washed and dressed, and propped upon some pillows on the floor.

'He's waiting for his breakfast,' the nurse exclaimed, a faint look of disapproval crossing her face at Caryn's lack of formality. 'If you'd like to come over here, I'll show you his menus for the day.'

Caryn had fed the baby his lightly boiled egg and cereal, and was assisting him to drink from his cup when Marcia came into the nursery. Half afraid their interchange the night before might have soured their relationship, Caryn was relieved to see the housekeeper smile warmly in her direction, although she reflected dryly that her affection was probably directed towards the child. But the tray she carried was not for Miss Trewen, who had already had her breakfast, and Caryn smiled her thanks as Marcia gestured that a car was downstairs.

'It's the taxi,' exclaimed the nurse eagerly, and when Marcia nodded, she looked pleased. Then she turned to Caryn: 'Now, you can manage, can't you? I haven't forgotten anything?'

'I did cope quite adequately until he was three months old,' Caryn pointed out patiently. 'But no, you haven't forgotten anything.'

The two women went out together, and Caryn grimaced at her nephew. 'Well,' she said encouragingly, 'it's just you and me, brother! Think we'll get along?'

Tristan laughed, showing a revolting mixture of milk and cereal rolling round on his pink tongue, but Caryn realised with a pang that she wasn't at all revolted.

After finishing his breakfast, Tristan lay on the rug and played for a while, while Caryn had hers. He lay there, reaching for his woolly duck and his rattle, shrieking his irritation when they persistently eluded his inexpert grasp. Then it was time for his nap, and rather than risk meeting either Melanie or her father downstairs, Caryn put him into his cot instead of taking him for the walk she would have preferred.

Still, the weather was definitely cooler today, and several spots of rain on the windows heralded a downpour. Caryn tidied up the nursery, put the rug and pillows and toys away, and then carried her tray downstairs to the kitchen.

Marcia was slicing runner beans into a saucepan, and smiled as she came in. Caryn put her dishes in the sink, waved away the housekeeper's protest, and washed them up herself. Then she turned rather awkwardly to her.

'Marcia . . . about last night . . .'

Marcia shook her head, and there was an air of finality

about the gesture. 'Forget it!' she mouthed silently, and Caryn decided she might as well.

She was on her way back upstairs when the front door opened and Tristan came in, brushing the droplets of rain from his zipped black windcheater. She had automatically paused when the door opened, but when she saw who it was, she quickened her step.

'Caryn!' His use of her name in the circumstances revealed his surprise at seeing her, and he came to the foot of the stairs, gazing up at her frowningly. 'I thought you were in London.'

She was in a quandary. After their last encounter, how could she behave towards him in a friendly fashion? It simply wasn't in character. And yet, remembering what she owed Bob and Laura—their sympathy and gentleness when Loren died, their friendship and companionship, their willingness to help with the baby—how could she turn her back on them when they needed her most? But what a position to be in, guessing the contempt he would display when he discovered what she wanted!

Now, she came down a stair and said stiffly: 'Miss Trewen wanted to spend the day with—with a friend. I offered to look after Tristan.'

His mouth thinned. 'There was no need for that. If you had told me, I would have arranged for Marcia to take over for one day. You didn't have to spoil your weekend.'

'Marcia has enough to do as it is. With—with your guests.'

His nostrils flared. 'We could have eaten out. That's no problem. I could have hired more staff.'

'It wasn't necessary,' she exclaimed, realising nervously that if she wasn't careful their conversation would degenerate into an argument. 'I didn't mind—honestly.'

'But you don't like looking after babies—you told me.'

Caryn drew an unsteady breath. 'Maybe I've changed my mind.'

'Why should you do that?'

'Oh, for heaven's sake, does it matter?' Caryn's fingers tightened round the baluster rail as she tried to control her impetuous tongue. 'I'm here now, and that's all that matters.'

'I should have been told.'

'I thought Miss Trewen had told you.'

'Obviously she didn't.' He regarded her broodingly. 'Well, as you are here, you can join us for dinner this evening.'

'I—don't think I can.'

'Why not?'

She hesitated, wishing desperately that he had entered the house just a few moments later. 'I—Tristan needs attention . . .'

His eyes rested disturbingly on her mouth. 'Don't we all?'

'Mr Ross . . .'

'Dinner,' he retorted harshly. 'At eight, Miss Stevens.'

During the afternoon, Caryn alternately sought to find reasons not to attend the dinner party or tried to justify her motives for going. If she did not join Tristan and his guests she knew she would anger him and while she knew he could not force her to go down, what better chance would she have of putting Bob's case to him? And yet wasn't that a foolhardy hope at best? Melanie was not likely to allow her escort out of her sight long enough to have a private conversation with him, and if the morning's encounter was anything to go on, he was not likely to listen to her anyway.

Baby Tristan had his tea at four o'clock, and then a bottle after his bath at six-thirty. He was just beginning to appreciate the benefits of being in water and Caryn was glad she had put on Miss Trewen's waterproof pinafore before tackling that particular task. Even so, she was hot and the floor was swimming with water before she managed to haul him out.

Dried and powdered and in his nightshirt, he smelled delicious, with that warm satisfying smell peculiar to babies. Curled on her knee, he took his bottle like an angel, and only began to protest when Caryn put him down to sleep.

'You mustn't be naughty tonight,' she told him severely, leaning over the tall side of the cot. 'Your Aunt Caryn has to go and put on her best dress and make polite conversation at a dinner party. Be thankful you're not expected to attend!'

Tristan settled down eventually, but not before making her later than she could have wished, and she had to forgo her bath and take a shower instead. Fortunately, she had chosen the dress she was going to wear during the afternoon, and it took very little time after her shower to put on her shreds of underwear and slide the clinging folds of the red silk jersey over her head.

It was a beautiful dress, she reflected, considering her mirror image, but perhaps a little bright for a simple dinner party. Still, she had no time now to change, and if Tristan didn't like it, he had only himself to blame.

She came down the stairs at a quarter to eight, and found Tristan and his guests having drinks in the sitting room. All eyes were turned in her direction as she came into the room, and just for a moment she allowed herself the satisfaction of knowing that her appearance compared favourably with Melanie's crystal blue chiffon. Then a burly, grey-haired man made his way towards her, and although he wasn't a lot like his daughter, she guessed this had to be Sir George Forbes.

'Caryn, isn't it?' he said, before Tristan could introduce them. 'Good of you to even the numbers. Pity you weren't here last night. Could have done with a bit of luck on my side.'

Conscious of Tristan's eyes upon her, Caryn allowed the older man to shake her hand, but she withdrew it firmly when he would have held on.

'Were you unlucky last night, Sir George?' she parried, keeping her smile in place, and he explained that they had attended a private gambling party.

'Do you like gambling, Miss Stevens?' Melanie asked silkily, but this time Tristan interposed,

'Caryn's an expert when it comes to games of chance, aren't you?' he asked, his eyes faintly hostile, and Caryn was glad when Sir George spoke again and she could evade a direct reply.

'Tris tells me your sister used to work for him,' he remarked, remaining uncomfortably close to her, and she nodded.

'Sherry?' suggested Tristan, attracting her attention, and awkwardly she nodded again: 'Thank you.'

'Tris fired her,' put in Melanie spitefully. 'Miss Stevens' sister, I mean.' She flicked a malicious glance at Caryn. 'She became—how shall I put it?—an embarrassment to him.'

'As you are now?' snapped Caryn impulsively, and saw the other girl's look of fury.

'Well said!' Sir George had obviously been imbibing quite freely already, and although Caryn's words had been unbearably rude, he took no offence at them. But Melanie did.

She turned to Tristan. 'Are you going to stand there and let that—that creature insult me?' she demanded, and his mouth thinned into an uncompromising line.

'As what she said was true, I don't see what I can do,' he retorted evenly. 'However,' his gaze flicked over Caryn contemptuously, 'I think she regrets saying it as much as you regret hearing it.'

Caryn's lips worked impotently for a moment, and she toyed with the idea of telling him exactly what she did think. But then common sense and discretion won the day, and she contented herself with a hard little look in Tristan's direction.

Dinner was served in the dining room. It was the first time Caryn had eaten in the impressive room that overlooked the drive at the front of the house. After the splendid views at the back, the front was something of an anti-climax, in spite of its boxwood hedges and flowering shrubs.

The meal Marcia served was delectable as usual. Prawns in aspic were followed by veal cutlets served with a sherry sauce, and there was a featherlight lemon soufflé to finish. Even Caryn, conscious as she was of Melanie's overt hostility and Tristan's brooding melancholy, could not resist trying everything, and the wine that accompanied the food relaxed a little of the tension she was feeling.

Marcia had brought in the cheese board when a car turned between the drive gates and cruised down to the door. Although it wasn't yet dark, it was impossible to see who it was from Caryn's position at the far side of the table, and Tristan's curt ejaculation made her think sinkingly of Dave O'Hara. But she was wrong.

'It's Angel!' he declared, thrusting back his chair and getting to his feet. 'Now why the hell couldn't she have let me know she was coming back today?'

'Angel?' Melanie's lips curved upwards. 'Oh, good!'

'Your daughter, Ross?' Sir George asked as Tristan strode towards the door. 'Good show!'

Only Caryn was unenthusiastic about the new arrival, and she thought cynically that if only Angela had arrived sooner she would have been spared the discomfort of this dinner party.

The front door was open and Tristan was helping the taxi driver to bring in his daughter's cases when Angela herself appeared, sleek and tanned after a month in the sun.

'Melly!' She and the other girl greeted one another eagerly, and Sir George had left his seat to go and join them.

'Sir George!' Angela exclaimed, leaving her friend to hug the older man, and Caryn could see the way Melanie's father's lips curled in anticipation. And why not? she thought dryly. In denim dungarees that accentuated the slender lines of her body, her silky blonde hair loose about her shoulders, Angela was the epitome of well-fed sophistication and unlike Caryn was more than willing to suffer his lustful glances. Her skin gleamed with the glow of good health, and only when she saw Caryn still seated at the dining table did her laughing good humour give way to sardonic irritation.

'Am I interrupting something?' she enquired of her father, who appeared at the door at that moment, having disposed of the taxi driver. 'I didn't know your secretary joined you for dinner, Tris. Or is this a special occasion?'

Caryn rose to her feet. She had had just about enough baiting for one evening. 'Your father invited me to make the numbers even, Miss Ross,' she declared stiffly. 'As they're odd again now, I'll solve the problem and leave you to drink my share of the coffee!'

'Now wait a minute——'

Angela's automatic retort was drowned by her father saying grimly: 'Sit down, Caryn!' but she ignored both of them.

'I'd really rather not,' she was beginning, and as if on cue, the baby's cry suddenly broke upon the awkward silence that had fallen. 'You see,' she got out huskily, 'duty calls!'

She had lifted her nephew out of his cot and was rocking him gently on her shoulder when she became aware of a shadow falling across them from the doorway. It had to be Tristan, and without turning, she said rather chokily: 'Please, go away! I can manage.'

'Oh, well, if that's how you feel . . .'

Miss Trewen's voice was affronted, and Caryn swung round guiltily, staring in bewilderment at the nurse. 'Miss Trewen, I . . .' She moved her shoulders helplessly. 'I'm sorry, I didn't know you were back. Oh, heavens, I didn't mean you!'

'My friend drove me back,' declared Miss Trewen, only slightly placated. 'I thought you must have heard me come upstairs.'

'No.' Caryn shook her head, unable to explain that she had been too depressed by the events of the evening to hear anything but her own erratically beating heart.

'Well, if that's the case . . .' Miss Trewen held out her arms. 'Let me take him. I think Mr Ross is looking for you.'

Caryn was tempted to hold on to the baby, but if it came to a choice between offending Miss Trewen and hiding her own misery, Miss Trewen would win every time. She passed the baby over to the nurse, and walked back into the nursery as Miss Trewen closed the bedroom door behind her.

The light in the nursery was harsh after the shadowy bedroom, and Caryn was blinking away a certain moistness when she realised she was no longer alone.

'Is he all right?'

Tristan straightened from his lounging position in the doorway, and came into the room. Watching him, Caryn wondered why it was that she should feel this overwhelming attraction for the man she had come here to hate!

'Miss Trewen's with him,' she replied tersely. 'Don't let us detain you. I'll wait and speak to her when she's settled him down.'

Tristan came to stand in front of her, looking down at her intently. 'Are you all right?'

'Why shouldn't I be all right?' she protested, smudging her hand across her cheeks. 'Oh, please, don't feel sorry for me!'

'Why not? What makes you so unique?' He hesitated, then he said huskily: 'It suited you, you know.'

'Wh-what suited me?'

'Having the baby in your arms,' he said surprisingly, and her head jerked up,

'You—saw—me?'

'From the doorway,' he conceded softly, and she knew she had not been mistaken in sensing his nearness. 'Then the good Miss Trewen appeared, and I got out of the way.'

Caryn's breathing quickened at his words, and her heart palpitated alarmingly. Close to him like this, his eyes were no longer harsh and cold, but warm and golden, like the sun, with all its heat.

'Caryn,' he said, and rather than look at him, she quickly turned away, knocking one of the baby's rattles from the table as she did so. She bent automatically to pick it up as he did the same, but instead of rescuing the rattle, his hands cupped her face, and then, with an urgent exclamation, his mouth was covering hers with all the warm emotion of which she knew he was capable. She straightened, her legs like jelly, and the kiss hardened and lengthened, parting her lips and drawing on the moist sweetness within. Her hands by her sides touched his hips, and their involuntary with-drawal was overridden by an almost compulsive need to feel him close to her. Her hands slid over him, and he shuddered as he gathered her closer, letting her feel the whole weight of his desire.

'*Tristan!*'

Melanie's voice drifted along the corridor from the upper landing, and with an abrupt movement Caryn was free, and Tristan was striding out of the nursery. Even as she stood there feeling that her whole world was caving in about her, she heard Melanie's light laugh, and with a crippled cry she ran to the door and slammed it behind him. So much for helping Bob and Laura, she thought bitterly. She couldn't even help herself.

In the morning, she felt no better. Instead, an intense awareness of impending disaster had descended upon her, and with cold reason she acknowledged that if she stayed here it was no longer just a possibility that she might become involved with Tristan. It was already too late for possibilities. Insidiously perhaps, against her will definitely, she was involved with him, and how could she betray her sister's memory by becoming the mistress of the man who had been the indirect cause of Loren's death?

She was in the nursery with Miss Trewen, having breakfast, when they had unexpected visitors. After the most perfunctory of raps at the door, Melanie and her father came in, and Caryn's sense of impending disaster magnified a hundred times. Why had they come here? Of what possible interest could baby Tristan be to them?

Miss Trewen, on the other hand, was flattered. She rose to greet them in something of a fluster, and Caryn's nails dug painfully into the palms of her hands.

'I hope you don't mind this intrusion, dear lady.' Sir George was at his most gallant, but his eyes flickered speculatively over Caryn's bent head. 'We're leaving this morning, and I felt we shouldn't go without introducing ourselves to the youngest member of the household.'

Miss Trewen glanced awkwardly towards Caryn then. 'Well, of course you're not intruding, Sir George. We've just had our breakfast, and we're having a little play on our rug before we have our nap.'

For once Miss Trewen's mannerisms failed to make Caryn smile. Glancing round, she encountered Melanie's vaguely mocking expression, and the other girl's lips curled contemptuously when she met Caryn's regard.

Sir George was accompanying Miss Trewen across to where the baby was lying kicking on his rug, and after another malicious look at Caryn, Melanie went after them. They stood looking down at the plump little legs kicking excitedly into the air, and Caryn suddenly wanted to rush across and snatch up the baby and hide him from their ungentle curiosity.

But it was too late. Sir George bent down towards Tristan, chucking him under the chin, and as the baby's face crumpled into a noisy objection, the man uttered a sound of surprise.

'Hey there!' he exclaimed, and Caryn waited apprehensively for him to notice the baby's resemblance to Tristan. For she had no doubt that the other girl had brought her father here for just this reason, although why Melanie should want to advertise the fact she couldn't imagine; 'Melly, doesn't he remind you of someone?'

Miss Trewen and Caryn exchanged a glance, and suddenly Caryn could sit still no longer. She slid off her chair, and as she did so Melanie gave a startled gasp.

'Yes!' she cried, and Caryn took an involuntary step towards her. 'Good lord! Dave O'Hara to the life!'

Caryn had never been so near fainting in her life. Her face

lost every scrap of colour, and she stared at the others with lips turning faintly blue.

Melanie straightened, and looked at her mockingly. 'Oh, dear,' she exclaimed spitefully. 'Didn't you see it? Tristan noticed it the first time he saw him.'

Caryn couldn't believe it. With a return of strength to limbs that had been temporarily paralysed, she rushed across the room, pushing Sir George aside with little ceremony, staring down at her nephew as if she'd never seen him before.

It was true! she thought sickly. And so many things fell into place. The feeling when she saw Dave that she had met him before, the fleeting resemblance she kept seeing in the baby that she had thought was Tristan. But she had seen Tristan in him because that was what she had wanted to see . . .

'I can see we've shocked Miss Stevens,' remarked Melanie lightly, but her father looked less self-satisfied.

'Look here, Caryn,' he said, half apologetically, 'I thought you knew. Melanie—well, I was led to believe that—oh, God! What a situation!'

Miss Trewen shifted uncomfortably, and belatedly Caryn realised that all this must be double-talk to her. Pushing back the weight of her hair with an unsteady hand, she tried to pull herself together, and taking pity on her, Sir George ushered his daughter towards the door.

'We'll—er—we'll be going,' he said, blustering himself a little now. 'Caryn, we'll no doubt see you again. Miss Trewen.'

He raised a hand in farewell, and the door closed behind them, leaving Caryn to make what explanations she could. But she wasn't ready for explanations. She needed time to think, not least about what this meant in terms of her own situation.

'I'm sorry, Miss Stevens,' Miss Trewen spoke uncomfortably, and Caryn quickly reassured her.

'Don't be. I guess it had to happen sooner or later.'

'But what's happened?' exclaimed the older woman anxiously. 'Who is this Dave O'Hara? Your sister's husband?'

'Oh, no. No!' Caryn put a hand to her throat, feeling sick. 'He's just—Dave O'Hara. Lead guitarist with Sweet Vibration.'

'What is Sweet Vibration?'

'A group. A pop group. You know—top ten, and all that.'

'And he's—Tristan's father?'

Caryn bent her head. 'Apparently.'

'You didn't know?' Clearly Miss Trewen was shocked now.

'No, I didn't know.'

'But——'

'I can't explain now,' muttered Caryn huskily. 'I can't. You'll have to give me time to absorb this. Then—then we'll talk.'

Miss Trewen sighed. 'Does this mean we'll be leaving here, Miss Stevens? I would like to know that.'

'What? Oh . . .' Caryn swallowed convulsively. That was something else she had to consider. 'I—I don't know. I just don't know . . .'

And with that Miss Trewen had to be content, but as she stumbled along to her own room, Caryn wondered how Loren could ever have lied to her as she had . . .

CHAPTER TEN

It was Monday morning, and no doubt Tristan was waiting to issue her instructions for the week, but Caryn lingered in her room, pacing the floor, hands pressed to her burning cheeks, unable to summon the courage to face him.

What did it mean? she asked herself again and again, and could come up with no satisfactory answer. Oh, it was simple enough to guess what had happened. She had only to remember Tristan's anger when he found she was with Dave to realise he was afraid of what might happen, but why hadn't he told her? And more importantly, why hadn't he told *Dave*?

And yet, thinking of the pop star and his life style, Caryn shuddered. Dave was a boy still, totally incapable of under-standing the needs of a baby. Was that why Loren had lied to her?

There was pain in that realisation. Whatever happened, whatever motive there had been behind this, Loren had lied to her. And if she had lied about one thing, had she lied about another?

But no! Loren had cared about Tristan Ross—Caryn was sure of that. She had talked of no one else all the time she was pregnant, and thinking of this another awful thought struck her. Could Loren have slept with both men? Could the child have belonged to either? Had she hoped it would be Tristan's? Was that why she had sent Caryn to him when she knew she was dying?

The whole situation was appalling, and Caryn wrapped her arms about herself closely, as if to protect herself from the dreadful repercussions of the Forbes' revelations.

Ultimately she knew she would have to speak to Tristan. By remaining in her room she was only putting off the evil day, and goodness knows, she had plenty to do. If the child wasn't his, then somehow she would have to take it away, but whether she could find another post where a child was welcome was doubtful. Of course, she could always apply to be someone's housekeeper. She had seen advertisements for such where 'one child' was not objected to. But what would the authorities have to say about that? She had only just managed to persuade them to let her keep Tristan, but the circumstances here were vastly different from the average housekeeping post. She pressed her lips tightly together. Laurence Mellor would say she had brought the whole thing upon herself, and it seemed so unfair that just when she was beginning to let herself believe that she was not going to be separated from the child, that unspeakable thing might happen. Unless Tristan wanted her to remain . . .

She thrust this unworthy thought aside. How could she let him go on supporting a child that was not his? How could she accept his—*charity*, for that was what it was?

He had known—she was convinced of that. So why had he done it? Pity? Guilt? *Christian charity!* There had to be more to it than that. He had had no love for Loren, he had shown that many times, so why had he taken it upon himself to give her son—and Dave O'Hara's—a home?

It was after nine-thirty by the time she summoned up the courage to speak to her employer, but when she reached the study she found only taped instructions waiting for her. Beside them was a note stating that he was driving Melanie and her father back to London, and nothing else.

She stared down at the note, blinking back the tears of pain and frustration that filled her eyes, and then sank down into the chair at her desk and buried her face in her hands.

Oh, God, she thought miserably, she didn't want to leave Druid's Fleet. Not because of her job—or baby Tristan's welfare; but because she loved Tristan Ross, against all reason . . .

'Where's my father?'

Angela's voice broke carelessly into her misery, and she raised her head dazedly to find Tristan's daughter standing squarely before her desk.

'Your father . . .' she said, somewhat stupidly, and Angela's arrogant features grew irritated.

'Yes. My father. Your employer, Tristan Ross. Where is he?'

Caryn pushed her fingers across her cheeks and held up her head. 'He—er—he's left for London.'

'He's what?'

'He's left for London,' said Caryn again, forcing her own troubles aside. 'He's driven Miss Forbes and her father back to town.'

'Damn!' Angela's mouth tightened. 'Damn, damn, damn! Now why the hell has he done that?'

Caryn couldn't answer her, so she remained silent, but Angela wasn't satisfied yet.

'I understood from Melanie that they expected to stay for a few days.'

Caryn hesitated. 'They—came on Thursday,' she said. 'They've been here four days already.'

Angela regarded her coldly. 'And you know nothing about it, of course.'

'What could I know?'

Angela looked as though she might say something, and then moved restively across to the windows. 'Tell me,' she said, with her back to Caryn, 'how much longer do you think you can stay here? How much longer is it going to take for you to realise that my father is only satisfying some ridiculous guilt he feels about getting rid of your sister?'

Caryn stiffened. 'What do you mean?'

Angela swung round, resting against the sill. 'Don't pretend you don't know what happened as well as I do.'

Caryn rose to her feet. 'If you'll excuse me——'

'No, I won't excuse you. And what's more, I think you ought to stop pretending you believe in this myth about Loren.'

Against her will, Caryn's attention was caught. 'What—what myth?'

'This myth of her being in love with my father. Loren wasn't in love with anybody, except perhaps herself.'

'You have no grounds——'

'I have every ground!' snapped Angela coldly. 'My God, do you think I couldn't see what game she was playing? Do you think I didn't know what was going on?'

'I think you were jealous!' declared Caryn tremulously, and as soon as the words were uttered, she realised how true that could be. Allan Felix had hinted that Angela considered Dave O'Hara her property. How galling it must have been for her to learn that he and Loren . . .

'Jealous!' Angela's face was contorted with anger now. 'Jealous! Of that little——' She used an epithet which made Caryn's colour pale. 'How dare you suggest such a thing? I had no need to be jealous of her. Tris wouldn't look at her. Not in a thousand years! Whatever sordid little details you have read about him, my father is a decent man, and no one can say otherwise. That's why your being here is so—so ludicrous——'

'I didn't mean your father!' declared Caryn unsteadily, prepared to defend Loren, whatever her faults. 'I meant Dave O'Hara!'

Angela uttered a shrill laugh. 'What?' she exclaimed disbelievingly. 'You think I'm jealous of you and Dave! My dear girl, if he's been friendly to you while I've been away, then believe me, that's only because I've not been around!'

'I don't mean me,' Caryn persisted, reflecting that either Angela was a very good actress or Allan had been totally wrong about her.

'Who, then?' Her eyes widened. 'Oh—you mean Loren!' Her lips curled. 'My God, we are scraping the barrel, aren't we? You don't honestly believe Dave cared about your sister, do you?'

Caryn stared at her, then she shuddered uncontrollably. 'You believe it was only—promiscuity, then?' She shook her head. 'I think you believe in myths too, Miss Ross.'

'What are you talking about?' Angela straightened away from the window. 'What do you know about anything?'

'I know—I know it takes two to—to—well, anyway, Loren's baby is alive and real—and no one, not even you, can deny that!'

'Why should I want to deny it? Just because your sister got herself pregnant and died having the child it doesn't make her some kind of saint, you know. Oh, I admit you fooled my father into thinking so, but you can't fool me! Just who was the child's father, by the way? I would like to know.'

Caryn stared at her through hollowed eyes. 'You mean—you mean——' Her throat worked convulsively, and Angela, alarmed by her pallor, came towards her.

'What is it?' she exclaimed. 'What's wrong? Oh, for the lord's sake, I'm sorry if I've upset you, but you must know, deep down, that Loren was not the little innocent you like to think her.'

Caryn shook her head, looking down helplessly at the

desk, and Angela actually placed a hand on her shoulder. 'Miss Stevens—Caryn! Heavens, calm down! Calm down! All I asked was——'

'I know—what you asked,' said Caryn chokingly, and suddenly comprehension dawned on Tristan's daughter.

'That's it, isn't it? she exclaimed, staring at Caryn. 'The child's father! You do know who it is, don't you?' She became impatient again. 'Well, come on—who is it? You'll have to tell me. I mean to know.'

Caryn sank down into her seat. 'I thought you knew . . .'

Angela's eyes narrowed, and now her hand fell to her side as she lost colour. 'You don't mean—I don't believe you!' She stared at Caryn, trying to get her to deny it. 'Dave? *Dave?* He—wouldn't do such a thing!'

Caryn made a helpless gesture towards the door, and with an ejaculation, Angela stalked out of the room and her footsteps could be heard as she ran along the corridor.

She was back in less than five minutes, and now her face was ashen. She looked at Caryn, and then with a moan, she dragged herself into her father's chair and burst into tears.

Caryn could find it in her heart to feel sorry for her. All her previous arrogance had disappeared, and now she was just a teenage girl whose boy-friend had been unfaithful to her. Realising there was nothing she could say to salve the pain she must be feeling, Caryn left the room, closing the door silently behind her.

In her own room, she stood blindly at the windows. No wonder Tristan had said Loren had been nothing but trouble from the moment she came here! No wonder he had dismissed her when he learned what was going on. Why had he done it? To protect Loren—too late as it turned out—or Angela, whom he obviously cared for deeply? Whatever his reasons, the pieces of the puzzle were falling into place now, and all that was left was his reasons for accepting Loren's baby into his home.

It might well be as Angela said. That he felt guilty for what happened. But nothing could alter the fact that Loren had used her working relationship with him for her own ends. She had known if she had come home to Caryn and told her that she was pregnant with the child of some pop idol, her sister would have felt little pity for her. Maybe she had even told Dave she was pregnant, and he had denied all knowledge of it. Maybe she had hung on in the hope that she might be able to persuade him to marry her, and when all else failed it was too late to get rid of it. There were so many maybes, so many possibilities, but what was becoming blatantly obvious was that Tristan's initial hostility towards her had been well warranted.

So now what could she do? She couldn't stay here. She couldn't accept Tristan's charity any longer. But she had no intention of going to the baby's real father and asking anything of him. So where did that leave her? Back with the possibility of a housekeeping post a long way away from Druid's Fleet . . .

Caryn arrived back in London in the late afternoon.

It had been surprisingly easy getting away. She had told Marcia that as Mr Ross was away she was going to drive up to town again to see a friend who was ill, and that she would ring as soon as she knew when she would be back. Miss Trewen, after her successful day out, saw nothing unusual in Caryn's departure, and as Angela was not around, Caryn left without difficulty. It wasn't entirely untrue, she consoled herself as she neared the suburbs of the city. Laura was not well, and she would find time to see her in between visiting employment agencies.

But she had no intention of taking advantage of Bob and Laura's hospitality, and the first thing she did on reaching London was to find a small hotel and book in for the night. Her room was small, and she had to share a bathroom, but at least it was clean and reasonably central.

It was too late then to start making the rounds of the agencies, so she visited a newsagent near the hotel and carried a copy of *The Times* back to her room. There was always the chance that she might find employment independently, and she had read these columns on other occasions with a wry smile.

First of all, she turned to the ordinary Situations Vacant columns. There were plenty of those, but most were professional vacancies, many of them overseas. It crossed her mind that she might enjoy working abroad, but taking a baby to a foreign country was always tricky.

She smiled as she saw the columns of secretarial posts. She wondered what those prospective employers would say if she turned up with a baby in her arms. No, secretarial jobs were out. At least, for the present.

But then one particular advertisement caught her eye. *Wanted*, it said, *personal, private secretary. Excellent position for qualified person. Apply: Dean Mellor, Lansworth College, Cricklewood.*

Laurence! she thought, in astonishment. Of course, his trip to the States must be over, and now he was advertising for a secretary before the new college term began.

It was strange how the thought of Laurence was comforting somehow. Perhaps because he was a link with her old life, the life she had once shared with Loren. She stared at the advertisement until the light in her room began to fade, and the unwelcome pangs of hunger overcame the misery she was feeling inside her.

Sleep, as was becoming usual these days, eluded her until

the early hours, and then she slept only shallowly, wakening when the wagons in a nearby railway siding began being shunted about by their handlers.

Over toast and coffee in the hotel dining room, she read the personal columns of the newspaper she had overlooked the night before. But there was nothing that appealed to her, and she left the hotel soon after nine, intent on covering as much ground as she could in the day. She left her overnight bag at the hotel, and was given the option of keeping her room for another night.

By five o'clock, her feet were aching, and the pounding in her head responded little to aspirins. She had visited no fewer than ten agencies, and although she had two possible interviews for tomorrow, neither of them particularly fitted the bill. One was as nursemaid to an Iranian oil executive's children, but the idea of living in such a place filled her with alarm. The other was less frightening: housekeeper to a widower in Coventry. But the agency thought he might well object to such a young child, and said that if Tristan had been three or four years older it would have been better.

She ordered a sandwich at the hotel and spent the evening in her room, resting her aching body. She knew she ought to ring Druid's Fleet, if only to ascertain that the baby was all right, but she was simply too weary.

In the morning, she tried to look on the bright side. Life in Iran might be fun, or alternatively the Coventry widower might like babies. She determinedly swallowed two slices of toast, because she was hungry, having had no dinner the night before, and after several cups of black coffee, set out again.

She was interviewed for the Iranian post at an hotel in Bond Street. When she arrived, however, there were at least twenty other girls waiting to be interviewed, and by the time she stepped across the thickly carpeted threshold of the suite the Iranians were occupying, she knew she had no chance of succeeding.

Her other interview was at the agency itself. A dour businessman spoke to her in a private office, and when Caryn told him she had the care of a five-month-old baby, he became quite angry.

'You did say you didn't object to a child,' she pointed out, with sinking heart, but he just opened the door.

'I said a child, not a baby!' he declared brusquely. 'Do you think I can do with sleepless nights and nappies about the place? No, I'm sorry, Miss Stevens, we were both misinformed.'

It was barely lunchtime when Caryn returned to the hotel. She had the addresses of several more agencies to try, but right now she hadn't the heart for it. Instead, she bought another copy of *The Times* and ate some lunch with it propped in front of her.

Laurence's advertisement was still there, like a baited hook to torment her. She wondered how many applicants he had had, and decided he would not be short of contenders. She sighed. If only Loren had never begged her to take her baby to Tristan Ross! She would, in all probability, still be working for Laurence, and the baby would have been adopted by some childless couple who would have given him a really good start in life. Instead, she had accused an innocent man of being its father, insinuated herself into his home, allowed the baby to wrap himself around her heart, and fallen in love with the one man who, because she was Loren's sister, thought she was easy game . . .

In the afternoon, she wondered what she should do. The idea of visiting Laura was attractive, but if Bob was there, how could she face him? She had promised to do what she could to help them, and had succeeded in helping nobody, not even herself.

Almost unthinkingly, she found herself getting on the bus to Cricklewood, but when she got off before the college she knew it had been her destination all along. She didn't know what she intended to do, but if Laurence was there she would speak to him, and maybe he would advise her as he had done in the past.

The college was strangely deserted. The students had not yet returned after the summer break, and only the maintenance staff and an occasional tutor walked the cloistered corridors.

Laurence's office was on the first floor, and Caryn was not stopped as she made her way up the wide marble staircase, and along the echoing hall. His secretary's office—her office, for four years—was empty, and she stood in the doorway staring at her desk. She had been happy here, she thought, although now she knew that there was another kind of happiness.

She was standing there, trying to summon up the courage to go and knock at Laurence's door, when she heard the sound of footsteps behind her, and glancing round, she saw her erstwhile employer traversing the corridor towards her, his black cloak billowing out behind him.

'Caryn!' Laurence exclaimed disbelievingly. 'Lord, it is you! Taylor said it was, but I didn't believe him!'

Taylor was one of the janitors, and although Caryn hadn't seen him on her way up, he was usually to be found about the place.

'Hello, Laurence,' she said, forcing a smile to her lips, but when she would have shaken hands with him, he brushed her outstretched arm aside and gathered her into an unexpected embrace.

'Caryn,' he said huskily. 'Dear Caryn! How lovely it is to see you!'

Caryn drew back, half in embarrassment, and he went past her to open the door of his office. 'Come in,' he invited. 'I'm not busy at the moment, although I shall be later. I've got half a dozen applicants coming to interview for your job.'

'I see.' Caryn licked her lips and followed him into his office, closing the door behind her. 'You're looking well, Laurence. Did you have a good trip?'

He moved his shoulders in a dismissing gesture. 'So-so,' he said, without emphasis. 'It's not a trip I would care to take again. Not alone, at least.' He paused. 'But you—how are you? I must say you're looking rather—tired.'

'I am tired,' Caryn admitted, sinking down into the chair opposite his desk. 'I've been trailing round London for the past two days, and I'm worn out.'

'Trailing round London?' Laurence Mellor frowned. 'Why?'

Caryn had taken the decision to tell him as soon as she got off the bus, and now she said quietly: 'I'm leaving—Mr Ross. It—well, it hasn't worked out as I planned. I'm looking for another post.'

Laurence gasped. 'Then look no further. Come back to me!' he said at once; as she had known he would.

Caryn bent her head. 'I couldn't do that, Laurence.'

'Why not?'

She looked up. 'You don't understand. I—I've been looking after Tristan—the baby, that is—for five months now. And I want to go on doing so.' She paused. 'It's as simple as that.'

Laurence looked disturbed. 'But I don't understand. How does that stop you from resuming your old job?'

Caryn sighed. 'Oh, Laurence! Do I have to spell it out for

you? I need someone to look after the baby as well as somewhere to live if I come back to you. And quite frankly, I—I
couldn't afford to employ anyone.'

Laurence absorbed this. 'So what is your intention? What
kind of post are you looking for?'

Caryn tried to sound objective. 'Well—a housekeeping
post, perhaps, or nursemaid to someone's children. Some
post where a baby isn't objected to.'

Laurence looked horrified. 'But you're not a nursemaid,
Caryn, or a housekeeper. You're a secretary—and a damn
good one!'

'Thank you.' Caryn managed a smile. 'You're very good
for my ego. But unfortunately, secretaries aren't usually
accompanied by dependants.'

'And have you had any luck?'

She shook her head. 'I had two interviews today—one
with an Iranian oilman, who said he would let me know,
and one with a widower from Coventry, who almost blew
his top when he found out how old Tristan was.'

'I see.' Laurence doodled absently on the pad on his desk.
'And—er—have you had any further thoughts about what I
asked you?'

Caryn frowned now. 'What you asked me? About going
to America, do you mean? But you've already been——'

'No, no! Not that.' Laurence sounded impatient. 'The
other thing I asked you. To marry me.'

Caryn caught her breath. 'But you weren't serious, Laurence,' she exclaimed. 'I mean, that was only an expedient for
the trip . . .'

He looked squarely at her. 'No, it wasn't. I might have let
you think so, I might even have thought so myself for a
while, but since you left, Caryn, I've realised I did mean
it.'

CHAPTER ELEVEN

'Oh, Laurence!' Caryn stared at him unhappily. 'We've had all this out before. You know I don't love you——'

'No. But I love you,' he said, shocking her into silence. 'I thought I'd never care for anyone else when Cecily left me, but it's not true. I do care for you, Caryn. I care for you a lot.'

Caryn got to her feet. She didn't know what she had expected coming here. Laurence's sympathy, perhaps, his understanding. Well, she had his sympathy, but anything else was out of the question. Maybe she had hoped he would offer to employ her and increase her salary, or alternatively offer her a job as *his* housekeeper. But telling her he loved her—she had not expected that.

'I'm sorry, Laurence,' she said. 'I—I don't know what to say.'

Laurence was on his feet and regarding her across the width of his desk. 'You should think about it, Caryn,' he said. 'Is it such a terrible thing to ask? Wouldn't it solve your problems, once and for all?'

'Wh-what problems?'

'Why, Loren's baby, of course. If you married me, he would at least have a decent start in life.'

Caryn pressed an uneasy hand to her throat. 'But I couldn't marry you for that!'

'Why not? People do marry for the oddest reasons, you know.'

Caryn shook her head helplessly. 'I'm flattered, of course.' She sought for reasons. 'Laurence, you don't even like children!'

'I've never had any. Perhaps if I had, my feelings would change.'

'You mean—you mean—*we* might have children?'

'Why not? I'm not too old, you know.' He sounded affronted, and she made an apologetic gesture.

'I know, I know. It's just that—oh, Laurence! You've rocked me on my heels!'

'Then think about it,' he said magnanimously, consulting his watch. 'But now, I'm afraid, my dear, I have to ask you to go. Whatever you decide, I still have these interviews to conduct.'

Caryn groped her way to the door.

'Of course,' he added, 'if you do—change your mind, that is—accept my offer, you'd be welcome to your old job back, if you wanted it.'

'And—and Tristan?'

'We could employ a nanny. I'm sure there are some excellent women around.'

Miss Trewen, thought Caryn dazedly. Miss Trewen could keep her job.

'Look,' said Laurence, 'you run along now. Where are you staying, by the way? I ought to have the address.'

'The White Feather. In Kensington,' replied Caryn, still in that dazed voice, and before she knew it, he had ushered her out into the corridor, and was telling her he would ring her there that evening.

But as she rode back to Kensington in the bus, Caryn's brain cleared. How could she contemplate marrying Laurence whatever the circumstances? He was too set in his ways, for one thing, and his words about having children had made her see that he would expect a real marriage, in every sense. It would solve her problems, of course it would, but did the end justify the means? She rather thought not.

What did disturb her was that she had even considered it. Before going to live at Druid's Fleet, she would never have left him in any doubt, whereas now, with two unsuccessful interviews behind her, she had actually weighed the pros and cons. Might Laurence even be able to persuade her if she saw him again? Might not desperation drive her to accept his offer?

She wished now she had not given him the address of her hotel. She should have told him she would ring him. That way, she was not committed. Not to anything.

On impulse, she checked out of the hotel when she got back, and left a message should a certain Mr Mellor call to tell him she would be in touch. Then she put her case into the boot of her car, and drove across town to Bloomsbury.

Parking in the narrow street was difficult, but eventually she managed to wedge the Renault between a hand-painted Mini and a grocer's van. Then she left her case in the boot, and ascended the two flights of stairs to Laura and Bob's flat.

Laura opened the door to her knock, but this was a vastly different girl from the one she had said goodbye to only five days ago. Now Laura's face was bright and cheerful, and although it sobered for a moment when she saw Caryn, the smile that lurked about her lips would not long be denied.

'Caryn!' she exclaimed, stepping towards her friend and hugging her tightly for a moment. 'Oh, Caryn, where have you been?'

'Where have I——' Caryn was beginning, when Bob's face appeared over his wife's shoulder, and with a sinking feeling she wondered if they imagined she was the bearer of good tidings.

'What an uproar you've caused!' Bob added to what his wife had already said, and then he came forward and shook her hand warmly. 'Caryn, I don't know how to thank you.'

This was all double-talk to Caryn, and she shook her head helplessly. 'I'm afraid I don't know what you mean . . .' she began, but they both drew her into the flat and the door was closed behind her before Laura tried to explain:

'Tristan Ross has been here,' she said, wrinkling her nose reprovingly. 'He's very worried about you. Have you seen him?'

Caryn's legs gave out on her and she sank down rather weakly on to the nearest chair. 'Tristan?' she breathed. Then more formally: 'Mr Ross!'

'Yes.' Bob took up the story. 'Apparently you just walked out on him for no reason.'

'No reason!' echoed Caryn disbelievingly. Then, realising explaining that remark entailed too many personal details, she added: 'What did he say?'

'What did he say?' Laura glanced sideways at her husband. 'Well, he said he was—extremely worried about you, and that if we saw you, we had to let him know immediately.'

Caryn's shoulders sagged. 'Is that all? Did he mention the baby? Is he all right?'

'Tristan junior is fine,' Laura assured her. 'Bob, go and put the kettle on, there's a love. I want to have a few private words with Caryn.'

'Okay.'

Bob grinned and marched into the kitchen, discreetly closing the door behind him, and the minute he had gone, Laura sat down opposite her friend and grasped Caryn's hand in hers.

'Now,' she said, 'let me thank you for—for speaking out for Bob. You don't know what this means to us, Bob getting a better job. It's like a dream. And I know—I just know he wouldn't have got it if it hadn't been for you. He told me what he'd said to you——'

Laura's words began by going over Caryn's head, but gradually the gist of them began to make sense. That job Bob was being interviewed for, he must have got it. And they thought it was all true.

'Oh, really, Laura . . .' she was beginning, when the other girl shook her head.

'Don't say anything,' she commanded. 'I know you're going to say it was nothing to do with you, but—well, we won't believe you, so forget it. But I just wanted you to know : . .'

If anything, Caryn felt worse. How could she stay here now accepting their hospitality on false pretences? Hadn't she had enough of that already?

'So . . .' Laura was speaking again, and Caryn came back to the present to hear her saying : '. . . so what did you walk out for? Mr Ross said he couldn't understand it.' She paused. 'And he was so cut up . . .'

Caryn's pale cheeks took on a rather hectic colour. 'It's a long story, Laura. The crux of it all is—Tristan Ross was not the father of Loren's baby.'

Laura's sandy lashes flapped incredulously. 'He's not!'

'No.' Caryn sighed. 'So you see, I can't stay there any longer.'

'But what will you do?'

'I don't know.' Caryn looked up as Bob came back into the room. 'Hmm, tea,' she smiled, glad of the respite. 'I could do with a cup.'

Laura looked by no means satisfied with Caryn's explanation, but the tea silenced them all for a while, and presently Bob took up the question of his new job.

'There were half a dozen of us,' he said, speaking for

Caryn's benefit, and making her feel so guilty. 'But all along, when I was being interviewed, I just had the feeling I was going to get it.'

'I'm so glad.' Caryn could at least be honest about that, and she had raised her cup to her lips again when there was a thunderous rapping at the door.

Laura started and looked at Bob, and he got frowningly to his feet. 'Who can that be?' he asked, looking at his wife, and in that instant Caryn knew. She put her cup down and rose to her feet, more nervous than she had ever been in her life before, and said clearly:

'It's Tristan!'

'Tristan!' Laura exchanged a glance with her husband, and then Bob had reached the door and was pulling it open.

'Mr Ross!' Caryn heard him saying, confirming her worst fears, and then Tristan had brushed past him into the room saying angrily:

'Where's Caryn? I know she's here. I saw her car outside.'

Caryn stilled her trembling lips by pressing them together and stepped forward. 'Here I am, Mr Ross,' she said stiffly, and then gasped when he came towards her and pulled her unresistingly into his arms.

'Where have you been?' she heard him say chokingly, burying his face in the hollow of her nape, and then he drew back to look at her as the sound of the kitchen door closing again signified that Bob and Laura had left them alone.

Caryn stared up at him uncomprehendingly, and thought inconsequently how haggard he was looking. But before she had time to formulate her thoughts, he spoke again.

'I've been out of my mind!' he muttered, his thumb probing between her lips. 'And if I hadn't had the idea of visiting Laurence Mellor this afternoon, I should never have thought of coming back here again.'

'You—you've seen Laurence...' she whispered faintly, and he nodded. 'But he didn't know I was coming here.'

'No, I know. He gave me the address of your hotel. But when I found that you'd checked out, I had the brainwave of trying here again, just in case you came to see Laura before leaving town.'

'I—I see.'

Caryn considered this tremulously while he continued to look at her, and then, very quietly, he said: 'Why in God's name did you run away?'

'I—didn't run away.'

'What would you call it?'

She trembled. 'After—after what happened, you must see I couldn't stay.'

There was silence for a moment, and then he said evenly: 'Why? What's changed? I knew Tristan was O'Hara's child from the beginning.'

'Then you should have told me!'

'Why? What good would that have done?' A moment's pause. 'Would you have believed me?'

Caryn drew herself away from him, unable to think with the hard muscles of his body touching hers. 'You—you may have a point there, but——'

'But nothing!' His expression hardened. 'I wanted you in my home, isn't that enough?'

'But why?' She stared at him.

'Why do you think?'

She didn't dare to think. 'I think this has gone quite far enough——'

'No,' he retorted, and now his voice was harsh and low. 'No, Caryn, it hasn't gone far enough!' and with hard determination he jerked her towards him again, and his mouth found the trembling weakness of hers.

He was not gentle with her. She could sense his impatience and his need to make her aware of him as he was aware of her, and despite all her efforts to evade him, eventually the probing pressure of his mouth forced hers apart, and then she was lost.

He kissed her long and expertly, caring little for their whereabouts, only making her want him as he undoubtedly wanted her. The fine material of his suit was no barrier to the thrusting urgency of his body, and she knew when she opened her eyes and looked into his that for once he was making no attempt to control the situation.

But at last he put her away from him, and raking his hand through his hair, he said: 'Do you have a coat or anything? We're leaving.'

'Tristan . . .' Caryn's hand fluttered to her temple. 'I—I——'

'We're leaving,' he repeated doggedly, and as if on cue, the kitchen door opened and Bob and Laura came slowly back into the room.

'Caryn . . .' Laura glanced awkwardly at her friend and then at Tristan. 'Are—are you going back to—to Wales?'

'No——'

'Yes!' Tristan's affirmation overrode Caryn's denial, and with a futile shake of her head, Caryn preceded him out of the flat.

Downstairs, she would have gone towards her car, but Tristan shook his head. 'I'll have that picked up later,' he declared tautly, and led her to the grey Mercedes, double-parked with a distinct disregard for any other road user. He opened the passenger side door, thrust her inside, and then walked round to get in beside her, and although she knew she ought to protest she remained silent.

They did not take the road west, however. Much to her

astonishment, Tristan drove into the heart of the city, and his concentration on other traffic curtailed any conversation they might have had. He drove through the park and turned into Park Lane, and finally brought the car into an underpass which turned out to be the underground garage for a huge block of luxury apartments. Of course, she thought nervously, Tristan had an apartment in town. Was that where he was taking her?

'Out,' he said unceremoniously, opening the door for her, and now she voiced her protest.

'I'm not going up to your apartment!'

'Aren't you?' His voice harshened. 'Do you want me to carry you?'

'Tristan——'

'Save it. The lift's over here.'

She went with him, telling herself they couldn't talk down here, but really only making excuses for her own traitorous behaviour. And yet it wasn't traitorous to feel as she did for Tristan, she thought miserably. Only stupid. Wasn't Loren's experience enough for her?

The lift swam up to the fourteenth floor with a smoothness that belied the effort. They emerged into a glass-roofed corridor, and she realised this was the penthouse suite. A panelled door had ROSS written in small gold letters, and then he had inserted his key and was pushing her before him into a wide green-carpeted hallway. Beyond was the huge living area of the apartment, but its plate glass and angled modernity was softened by warm colours and antique furniture. There was even a fireplace, surely only ornamental, that helped to create the illusion of age that was amazingly not out of place in these contemporary surroundings. Bookshelves, a writing bureau, a gate-legged table with claw feet; and lots of soft armchairs and cushions invited relaxation.

Caryn walked into the middle of the floor, having registered all these things at a glance, and stood there waiting for Tristan to speak to her, feeling rather like one of the Christians in the arena at Rome. Tristan himself seemed in no hurry now he had her there, and closed the living room door with a definite click, before strolling slowly towards her.

'Now,' he said huskily, 'shall we take up where we left off?'

Caryn backed away from him. 'It's no use,' she declared unevenly. 'I know you've—you've been very kind to me—to the baby—but it's over.'

'You're wrong,' he stated, but he made no effort to go after her. 'It's only just beginning.'

Then he sighed and indicated one of the comfortable chairs. 'Won't you sit down? I'm afraid I can't offer you tea, my housekeeper here only comes in when I need her, and she didn't know I would be needing her today. But there's—sherry, if you like. Or something stronger?' He raised his eyebrows.

Caryn shook her head, and when she still continued to hover by the fireplace, Tristan turned away and walked across to the windows.

'Suppose you tell me what happened,' he said. 'How did you find out about—about the child being O'Hara's?'

Caryn gasped. 'You know!'

'I know?' He turned to face her, hands behind his back. 'I assure you I don't. Unless . . .' He paused. 'The resemblance is beginning to appear, I admit . . .'

'No!' Caryn shook her head. 'Your—your—Melanie pointed it out.'

'Melanie!' Now she really had his attention, and judging from the way his nostrils flared, she did not envy Melanie's next interview with her—her—her what? Caryn hesitated. Her fiancé, perhaps? She inwardly winced. He was too old to be called her *boy*-friend.

'What did Melanie say exactly?' His voice was cold now, but she had to go on.

'She—she and her father—they came to the nursery.'

'When?'

'The—the morning they were leaving.'

'What!' He stared at her. 'You mean—they actually told you in front of Miss Trewen?'

'They didn't so much tell me as—as recognise the likeness.'

Tristan's lips tightened. 'Melanie knew whose child he was. I told her.'

Caryn said nothing, and he took a deep breath. 'And that was why you left?'

Caryn frowned. 'How did you know I knew if Melanie didn't tell you?'

'Angela told me.'

'Oh! Angela.'

'I gather you had quite a *tête-à-tête* with her.'

'I wouldn't call it that exactly. I'm sorry, I didn't know she didn't know—Oh, that sounds awful. What I mean is——'

'I know what you mean. I was going to tell her myself when she got back. After—after that business with O'Hara——'

'What business with O'Hara?'

'Him taking you to St Gifford. I warned him to stay away from you.'

'You did—what?' The words came out very faintly.

'I warned him to stay away from you. I had some people

in for drinks one Sunday, and I used it as a pretext to get him there and tell him.'

'I see.' Caryn caught her lower lip between her teeth. That must have been the so-called party Dave had mentioned. Was that when he had had the idea to come back to Port Edward and date her? Because Tristan had warned him off? But then if it hadn't been for what he had said about Melanie, she would probably never have gone with him.

'Anyway,' Tristan went on, 'I decided I'd put up with his ways long enough.' He sighed. 'Angel was mad about him, you see, and I guess I tried to find excuses for him because of that. I guessed something was going on between him and Loren, and that was part of the reason why I fired her. I didn't know it was already too late.'

Caryn digested this with difficulty. 'And—and you knew——'

'—right from the start,' he agreed heavily.

'But—but why let me stay?'

'I told you at the Westons' apartment.'

Caryn's cheeks flamed. 'I—I'm not like Loren. Whatever you may think, I—I'm not like her . . .'

'What are you talking about?' He came towards her, and she knew this was where she had to stand and fight. 'What has Loren to do with us?'

'I—I won't—that is, I know you can make me, but I won't stay with you——'

His hand over her mouth silenced her with a gulp. His eyes were darker now, darker and strangely angry. 'What in hell do you think I'm saying?'

She made a muffled sound, and impatiently he released his hand. 'I—I don't sleep with men,' she got out jerkily, and a faint smile touched his lips.

'You said that once before,' he said, taking her by the

shoulders and drawing her resisting body towards him. 'And I said you would. Don't you think husbands and wives should share the same bed? Or is that another of your funny little quirks?'

'Hu—husbands and wives?' she stammered. 'What do you——'

'What do you think I mean?' Impatience coloured his tone again. 'For God's sake, Caryn, I'm asking you to marry me! There! Is that clear enough for you?'

Caryn reached up and touched his face. 'You—mean it!'

He turned his mouth into her palm. 'Let's say I can't go on taking cold showers,' he murmured huskily, and her arms slid completely round his neck.

Their hunger for one another could not be assuaged with mere kisses, and eventually Tristan pulled her down on to his knees on one of the low armchairs, saying half grimly: 'There are still things that have to be said.' He hesitated. 'About Loren . . .'

Caryn buried her face in his shoulder. 'Angela told me a little about her, and I believe her, but I don't think she was as black as she's been painted.'

Tristan sighed, his lips against her temple. 'No,' he agreed, speaking against her skin, 'but she did—disrupt my household. She and O'Hara both.'

'And you?' Caryn murmured softly.

Tristan's fingers absently caressed her throat. 'Yes, me,' he said flatly. 'I've asked myself what my part in it all was, and I honestly can come up with no satisfactory answer. I know she saw working for me as a sort of glamorous occupation, and I guess the presence of groups like Sweet Vibration added to her delusions. But I don't honestly think she saw me as anything but an employer until after that affair with O'Hara. Then, when it became obvious that there was no chance that he'd marry her, she turned her attention to me. I guess that was when I knew she'd have to go.'

'When she came back to London, she talked of no one but you.'

'A defence, I suppose. Or maybe she intended coming back and—well, asking me for money.'

'Blackmailing you, you mean?'

Tristan shook his head. 'Nothing so serious. Loren was not really bad, only irresponsible.'

Caryn pressed herself closer. 'Thank you for saying that.'

Tristan bent his mouth to hers and then, when their lips clung, he drew back again. 'So—then you came to me, threatening all manner of things, and what happened? I suddenly found myself wanting to help you—to make up to you for what happened to Loren. I didn't realise until later exactly how small a part Loren played in my feelings for you.'

'But you never said,' Caryn protested, and his hand slid along her thigh.

'Would you really have listened to me? Wouldn't you just have thought I had some ulterior motive? I wanted you to get to know me, to like me, before I showed you how I felt.' He shook his head. 'That day you were late back from the beach—God, I could have killed you then! Falling asleep in some cove where the tide could have come in . . . And I was searching every cove I knew trying to find you!'

'Oh, Tristan!'

'You may well say "Oh, Tristan". You've given me some pretty hairy moments.'

'Like the night I rang you from St Gifford?'

'Like the night you rang from St Gifford,' he agreed.

'But you came back early both times. You weren't expected.'

'I couldn't keep away from the place,' he muttered, burying his face in her hair. 'Or you! Don't you know right now I should be at the studios recording tomorrow evening's programme?'

'But, Tristan——'

She would have sat up, but he pressed her back, his mouth curving sensually. 'Stay where you are. This is far more important than any television programme.' His lips parted. 'So—will you marry me? And soon? I don't think I can wait much longer.'

Caryn lifted her shoulders. 'But Melanie . . .'

'What about Melanie?'

'I thought—that is—she calls you darling.'

'Melanie calls everybody darling.' He smiled. 'Did she make you jealous? That was the idea.'

'Tristan!' She sat up to stare down at him. 'It wasn't!'

'It was. Melanie's really a friend of Angel's. Didn't you guess?'

Caryn shook her head. 'Then why did she reveal whose baby it really was?'

He gave a mocking smile. 'Well, I'm not saying that perhaps Melanie didn't have ideas of her own,' he teased, and Caryn dug her elbow into his ribs.

'I can hardly believe this,' she said tremulously. Then, with feeling, she said: 'I'm so glad things have worked out for Bob and Laura, too.' She smiled reminiscently. 'He's going to work for Area-South television as well.'

'I know.'

Tristan's reply was laconic and she looked sharply at him. 'How do you know? Oh—they told you.'

'No.'

Tristan shook his head, and mystified, Caryn frowned.

'Then how did you——' An idea dawned. 'Did you know he was having an interview?'

Tristan nodded. 'Warmer,' he agreed. 'I recognised the name, and the address.'

'But did you . . .' She hesitated. 'That is . . . Bob asked me . . .'

'. . . to intercede for him?'

'With you. Yes.'

'I thought he might. That was one of the reasons why I suggested you came to London last weekend. Besides, you needed the break.'

'But why did you want Bob to speak to me?'

He shrugged. 'I wanted you to have to come to me and ask me for something. I guess I wanted to show you I wasn't the brute you imagined me to be.'

'I didn't really imagine that,' confessed Caryn honestly. 'From the very beginning, I had to fight against being— attracted to you.'

'That sounds more interesting,' he murmured huskily, and there was silence in the apartment again.

'Miss Trewen will be pleased,' murmured Caryn drowsily at last.

'Mellor won't,' remarked Tristan, not without some satisfaction. 'When I saw him this afternoon, I told him I loved you and that I was going to marry you. He said you were considering his proposal.'

'Poor Laurence!' Caryn kicked off her shoes and curled her legs about Tristan's. 'I shouldn't have gone to see him.'

'Well, I'm glad you did,' retorted Tristan. 'What on earth have you been doing anyway?'

'Trying to find another job. One where they would take a baby.'

'Oh, Caryn . . .' Tristan's fingers unbuttoned her shirt and his mouth sought the rosy peaks exposed to his gaze. Then, with a sound that was half groan, he lifted her into his arms and deposited her in the armchair he had just vacated.

'I can't go on holding you without——' He broke off abruptly. 'I think we'd better go out for something to eat. Unless you want to drive back to Wales tonight.'

'Is Angela expecting you to return?'

'Angel hopes we return together. After what I told her, she knows if we don't, her life won't be worth living.'

'Poor Angel!'

'Angel will survive, she's that kind of person. Myself, I'm not so sure . . .'

Caryn frowned. 'Will you tell Dave about—about the baby?'

'Some day, perhaps,' Tristan replied thoughtfully. 'I don't know. Maybe we can give him a better home than O'Hara ever could. And at least he'll have brothers and sisters . . .'

'I wonder what Marcia will think.'

'Marcia will be pleased. She likes you, you know that. And having the baby about the place has made a tremendous difference to her.'

Caryn nodded. 'It must have been a dreadful experience for her, losing her own family like that. Do you think she will ever speak again?'

Tristan's face looked grim for a moment. 'When I met her she was in the local hospital, recovering from the attack. They cut her tongue out, you know. That's why she doesn't speak.'

'Oh, Tristan!' Caryn was appalled. 'How ghastly!'

'It was—at the time. It still is, I suppose. Except that now she's adapting to her new life. It's two years since her husband was killed. Life has to go on.'

'Yes.'

Caryn absorbed this silently, then, noticing his rather strained expression, she uncurled herself from the chair.

'Do you want to go out?' she asked, and Tristan's tawny eyes grew dark.

'No,' he admitted softly. 'I want to love you. I want to show you what making love really means. But I've no intention of shocking that prudish little mind of yours any more than it's already been shocked, so we'll go out.'

Caryn came towards him and wound her arms round his neck. 'What if I told you I was suspending my rule about sleeping with men?' she murmured.

'Well, so long as the suspension only applies to me, I'd go along with that,' he agreed huskily, and gathered her fully into his arms.

Best Seller Romances

Romances you have loved

Mills & Boon Best Seller Romances are the love stories that have proved particularly popular with our readers. They really are "back by popular demand." These are the six titles to look out for this month.

LOREN'S BABY
by Anne Mather

Caryn just couldn't be sure whether or not Tristan Ross was the father of her dead sister Loren's baby. Surely Loren had been telling the truth? Tristan denied it – yet he was making himself responsible for the child, wasn't he? And then Caryn found herself faced with another problem . . .

REEDS OF HONEY
by Margaret Way

Frances returned to her grandfather's plantation in the north of Queensland with only the hazy recollections of childhood to guide her future actions. Should she marry her cousin Dario and ensure that the name and fortunes of the Donovans survived? It was her decision. So why did the arrogant Scot Sutherland have to interfere?

Mills & Boon

BEWILDERED HAVEN
by Helen Bianchin

...nny thought Zachary Benedict was the most conceited man ...e had ever met, and she had no intention of becoming yet ...other of his long string of conquests – and anyway, after Max ...e didn't want to get involved with *any* man again. But Zachary, ...r reasons of his own, pursued her relentlessly. Surely she ...ouldn't find herself weakening?

THE MATCHMAKERS
by Janet Dailey

...rdan Long considered that Kathleen Darrow was far too ...ung for the job of companion to his two young daughters – but ...e girls liked her far and away the best of all the candidates for ...e post. So they put their heads together and hatched a plot . . .

MASTER OF COMUS
by Charlotte Lamb

...r the sake of her family's fortunes Leonie had agreed to an ...ranged marriage with her cousin Paul – whom she had always ...ro-worshipped anyway. But Paul had never been a ...e-woman man, to put it mildly – and nothing about his ...haviour suggested that marriage had changed him . . .

THE MARQUIS TAKES A WIFE
by Rachel Lindsay

...rke Powys, fourteenth Marquis, was more interested in ...search work in Africa than in settling down at his seat and ...oducing an heir – much to his grandmother's distress. So she ...nt to join him in Africa with her young companion Beth ...iller, to see if she could talk him round. In the process Beth ...came involved with the Marquis's romantic life and was ...tounded when he asked her to help him fight off two ...fferent women!

the rose of romance

YOURS absolutely FREE
Mills & Boon
Catalogue

We know you enjoyed this Mills & Boon Romance. So we'd like to tell you all about the whole range of other exciting titles we offer – titles we know you wouldn't want to miss!

The Mills & Boon Catalogue offers you a fantastic selection of Romantic fiction written by the world's leading authors. Longer Romances offering you nearly four hundred pages of passion and intrigue. Dr/Nurse Romances for a truly romantic look at the world of medicine and our Masquerade Series to whisk you away to bygone ages. There is also a selection from our Romance Series, PLUS a whole range of exciting bargain book offers!

What are you waiting for? For your FREE Mills & Boon Catalogue simply complete and send the coupon to:– MILLS & BOON READER SERVICE, P.O. BOX 236, THORNTON ROAD, CROYDON, SURREY, CR9 3RU, ENGLAND. OR why not telephone us on 01-684 2141 and we will send you your catalogue by return of post.

Please note:– READERS IN SOUTH AFRICA write to Mills & Boon Ltd., Postbag X3010, Randburg 2125, S. Africa.

– – – – – – – – – – – – – – – – –

Please send me my FREE Mills & Boon Catalogue.

NAME (Mrs/Miss) _____ EP5

ADDRESS _____

COUNTY/COUNTRY _____

POSTCODE _____

BLOCK LETTERS PLEASE